FINDING LOVE

ELITE MAFIA OF NEW YORK SERIES
BOOK 3

MISSY WALKER

To Andy,
You were right. Nothing great is ever given, it's earned.

1

LUCA

Desperate.

I don't recall *ever* feeling this way.

Frantic.

It's rare for me even to think this word.

Insanity.

This shit is all the fuck around me.

It was stupid and careless of me to consider we were safe in the damn Hamptons.

All I wanted was for Emilia to have a normal week away from the restraints of the family compound—those bland stone walls blocking out the world.

I blink away the burning of my tired, scratchy eyes and stare at the familiar faces standing in my father's office. "Somebody give me some good news!" I grunt out the words in a bad-tempered tone, my upper lip curling in disdain at the ineffectual assholes in front of me.

Men in my position do what's best for the people they love, even if it means upsetting them. Emilia might have loathed me for forcing her to stay here—where I knew she would be safe—

but all I needed was for her to be exactly that. *Safe.*

Now look where that's got me.

Emilia is in a hospital bed.

And she has no memory of anything that's happened between us.

I'm a damn stranger. *Again.* One she fears and probably resents.

And considering all I've ever done is cause her pain, she may be right.

My father sighs deeply before glancing around the room as I did. My brother, Dante, looks roughly as well rested as I'm sure I do—the dark circles ringing his eyes speak of days spent shaking every tree, accessing every bit of intel he can gather about the man who put Emilia in the hospital after leaving her for dead. He is slumped in a leather club chair in front of Papa's desk, his head propped on one hand.

My cousins, Niccolo and Francesco, are weary, standing with their backs against the bookshelves lining one wall. They returned from their patrol, for lack of a better word, only minutes ago after spending the night combing the streets for any sign of Alessandro Vitali or one of his close associates.

When no one offers an answer, my father shrugs. "I wish I had good news for you. We're still looking for him, but he's gone underground."

Cesco flexes his right fist, where I now notice traces of dried blood along his knuckles that hint at his interrogation methods. "Word on the street is he's holed up with some bitch he keeps a secret." Disdain drips from his every sylla-ble, and I have to agree. Hiding behind a woman like a fucking pussy after leaving another woman for dead is just the type of scum Alessandro is.

Pain grips its way around my chest, suffocating me when

I think about what he could have done to my poor Emilia if we didn't get there in time.

I know he's turned into a ghost, of course, though who could blame me for hoping we'd find him and crush his skull to powder? But that won't change things right now.

I can't live without Emilia.

I can't force her memory to return.

There's nothing to do but blindly grasp in the dark for some hint of light. Hope. I should know better by now.

I rake my hand through my messy hair and let out a heavy sigh. "Thank you for the update," I offer as I stand, stifling a groan when my tight muscles ache at the slightest effort. "I'm headed back to the hospital."

"Are you sure that's a good idea?" When I shoot my father a glare, he holds up his hands in surrender. "I'm asking for her sake. I know you feel like you have to be with her, but forcing yourself on Emilia isn't helping her memory return."

Resentment bubbles in my chest. He sounds like my mother, who gave me the same bullshit last night after bullying me into coming home for a few hours. The thought of them talking behind my back leaves me gritting my teeth. "I'm not forcing anything on anyone. But I'm going to be there for her whether she wants me there or not." I can't pretend the nights I've spent on a cramped sofa have been comfortable or restful, and it's not like I got any rest last night, either. The same meager nightmare plagued me.

Those nightmares follow me down the hall of my family home, taunting me with every step I take.

My fault.

All my fucking fault.

Sometimes, in those dreams, I find her dead. Other times, I hear her screams and the sound echoes in my head long after I've woken up. It's echoing in my head now—her pain and terror.

Vinny is waiting for me when I step outside, where I can almost taste snow in the air. I barely feel the cold that quickly penetrates my button-down, and it doesn't occur to me until I'm in the car that I forgot to put on my coat before leaving. What does it matter?

I growl and grit my teeth at my own weak, pathetic thoughts. Emilia has never needed me more than she does now, even if she doesn't know it yet. She will soon. I have to believe she will. I can't let her find me exhausted and sick when she does.

The first snowflakes land on my shoulders once I exit the car and hurry into the hospital. It's been five days since we first rushed Emilia through these doors, I know the layout like the back of my hand. I don't bother going through the motions of checking in with the front desk staff or getting a stick-on name tag. They know better than to try to stop me on my way to the bank of elevators, one of which I step into before pressing the button for the top floor.

The guards are changing shifts when I arrive. "How is she?" I ask Massimo, who was arriving as I was leaving for home last night.

"Just woke up maybe an hour ago. The roses you ordered got here before that." He barely stifles a yawn before leaving while Bruce takes his place on a folding chair outside Emilia's door. His brother, Bruno, was murdered in the guest house the night of Emilia's kidnapping, so he takes his duty seriously. It's personal for him. No doubt he wishes one of Vitali's guys would come along so he could have his pound of flesh in return.

Rather than enter through the door to the family waiting room on the other side of the suite, I open the one to Emilia's room to say good morning. Oddly enough, it's one of the things I miss most—something as simple as wishing her a good morning, basking in the warmth of her sleepy smile, and watching her return to life after hours spent resting in my arms.

How was I supposed to know it would all end so suddenly? That I'd go back to being the enemy, someone to fear and dread?

I have to pretend not to notice the way she stiffens and draws the blankets closer to her chin as soon as she sees me. "Good morning," I offer with a grin. "I heard your flowers arrived. What do you think of them?"

How can she look so much like the Emilia I left for what I thought would only be an hour? Granted, there are changes, starting with the uneven tufts of hair left behind after the Vitali crew crudely chopped most of it off. Then there are the slowly healing bruises and lacerations to her face. The sight of them sickens me, not because of the damage they do to her perfect beauty, but because they, too, serve as a reminder of how I failed her. I should be the one whose face looks like a punching bag, not her. She's never done a single thing in all her life to deserve what happened to her.

All she did was love me.

"Roses are my favorite." She won't look at me, focusing her attention to the lush blooms arranged in a crystal vase on the bedside table. I can let that go since the twitching of her lips is more important. The way she smiles softly, looking at the flowers.

I still have the power to bring a smile to those bruised lips.

"How are you feeling today?" Fuck, this is so awkward. I've been inside this woman. I was minutes from asking her to marry me the night she was taken. I've envisioned our life together so many times the future seems more real than the present.

Yet here we are, strangers to each other.

She glances away from the blooms before averting her gaze again. "I was watching the news earlier. I saw you on TV. Now I know where I recognize you from."

Goddammit. "What did you see?" I ask, approaching the bed, one slow step at a time.

"Something about violence between your family and another," she explains. "Vitali, the name was. I recognized that too. From work, I guess." She lifts a shoulder, her voice flat and emotionless. "So, at least I understand that much. How I knew your face."

What am I supposed to do? Congratulate her? Tell her I'm glad? Once again, I'm torn between patiently loving her and desperately needing her to love me, this constant back-and-forth, push and pull. It's infuriating, but I can't show her my fury.

"Is there anything you want to ask me?" I ask, fighting to be gentle as I sit on the edge of the bed. She sucks in a sharp breath through clenched teeth, but I won't get up when it's her nearness I need most. I can't stay away. "Whatever it is. I'll do my best to help you remember."

She's considering the idea. Her memory of the past few months might have vanished, yet some things don't change. She's as easy to read as ever. "No," she finally decides, drawing her knees close to her chest when my hand drifts too close to her leg.

The bitter bile of rejection rises in my throat, leaving me fighting to maintain composure as I draw my hand back. There's no way in the world she doesn't remember how useless it was to deny our connection. Fuck, I tried to deny it myself, yet I had no choice but to threaten to turn my back on my entire family if it meant protecting her life.

"You mentioned work," I prompt. "You remember your job?"

Her twitchy fingers work the blanket's hem, almost compulsively picking at a loose thread. Anything, so long as she doesn't have to look at me. "Sure. I mean, mostly. I know I have a partner, but I can't picture them. I can't remember the last case I worked on. I need to get back to it," she points out. "They have to be wondering why I haven't called. Why don't I have a phone in this room? Why can't I have my cell?"

This again. Like my answer is going to change. "I told you already. It's complicated," I murmur as gently as I can when what I want to do is scream.

I should be glad to see the anger that flashes across her face. It means she's stronger. Why does that strength have to be directed at me? "Letting the people who know me know I'm alive is complicated?" she snaps.

And I thought it would be a good thing to visit her. This is the first time she's dared to make a demand of me. I should be glad she's feeling strong enough, but that's the furthest from my mind. "You're not missing anything, I promise. Besides, the doctors didn't think it would be a good idea," I remind her. "There's too much missing from your memory, and you might not be able to process everything coming at you all at once."

"Like what? You threw yourself at me when I first woke up, and I had no idea who you were. Today, I found out you're a member of a mafia family." She spreads her arms. "I'm still alive and breathing, right? That didn't break me, did it?" The defiance in her voice reminds me of what first drew me to her, besides a body I'd give anything to touch again. Her attitude has never failed to turn me on, and the present moment is no exception.

I'm burning to put this bed to use.

Maybe then, she'd remember me.

Us.

"For all you know," I counter as quietly as I can. "It might have set you back when I startled you. Your team said you need to be careful."

"Why do they speak to you but not to me? Isn't that a violation somehow?" she demands, lifting her chin. Fuck me. I'd give anything to kiss the defiance away until she melts in the heat.

"They know how important your care is to me. I brought you in after you were hurt." It's not easy remembering that night—the helplessness, holding her, and feeling like she was slipping away no matter how tightly I clutched her.

The entire team knows better than to address anybody but me when it comes to her condition. No one outside these walls is to know she's a patient. No calls to family. Besides, I'm her family. They go through me and me alone.

"And how..." her voice wavers and cuts out, but she pushes through like the warrior she is, "... how do I know it wasn't *you* who hurt me?"

It takes everything I have not to flinch under her simple question. Never has innocence pierced me the way hers does now. "You need to trust me, Emilia. All I ask for is your trust."

"You won't let me have a phone, and I'm supposed to trust you?" She sinks against her pillows with a weary sigh, like sitting and talking with me is too much. "I'm sorry, but you're asking a lot."

As much as I loathe it, there's no choice but to tell her

the most convenient part of the truth. "You aren't a detective anymore. You resigned weeks ago."

"Bullshit," she blurts out in a trembling voice as the color drains from her cheeks. "I would never."

"You did." Gesturing toward her right arm, I explain, "You have a scar there now. You were shot in the arm and suffered nerve damage."

She doesn't want to believe me. I see it in the way she flexes her hand and winces as she lifts the sleeve of her flowered gown to examine the small yet very visible scar left behind. "You were shot by a man we assumed was already dead," I murmur as she studies herself. "It was my fault you were hurt. I should have made sure he was dead. I'll never forgive myself." Truer words have never been spoken.

"So I quit my job?" Her voice is soft, like a little girl who's lost her way and doesn't know what to believe or where to go now. Here I am, ready to take her by the hand and guide her, and I'm the last person she'd rely on.

"You did." I'm trying like hell to ease her into it. Gentleness isn't my strong suit. I don't have a lot of practice with it, let alone patience.

Her baby blues are full of apprehension when they meet mine. "Where do you come into this? You knew what I do... did... for a living, but we were still together?"

I've had days to consider how I'd explain everything, yet words escape me. It could be that no amount of imagination could possibly prepare me for being in her presence. She won't let me touch her, yet I can see her. Smell her. Feel the warmth radiating from her trembling body. Her presence is too powerful, and I came too close to losing her to do anything but yearn for her now.

Emilia needs me to be stronger than that.

Swallowing back my longing, I murmur, "It's a very long

story. All I can do is ask you to trust me. Believe me when I tell you we were together, and we were happy. Vacationing in the Hamptons, having a great time." Another swallow, this time to clear the lump in my throat. "Planning a future together."

That's what does it. She flinches at the word future, frowning, her brows drawing together. "My head hurts. I need to rest now." Without another word, she turns, facing away from me, ending the conversation by revealing the stitches running along the back of her head—twelve in all, and every one of them a silent condemnation.

"I'll let you rest, then. But I'll be in the other room if you need anything." She offers no response, only pulling the blanket over her shoulder and tightening into a ball.

This is the way she acts when she knows nothing but my name. How much worse will it get when she remembers how we met? Her determination to build a case against me and my family?

I can't let that happen. She needs to love me again before she remembers more, or she needs to remember everything all at once. Since the medical team believes her recovery will take time, the former seems my only path to salvation.

I have to make her love me.

Considering I don't know how I managed it in the first place, I'm fucking lost and more determined than ever to find Vitali and end his miserable life before wiping his entire family off the map. Nobody takes what belongs to me.

But killing him won't bring her back, and that matters more than anything because I need her more than I've ever needed anything. I was born to be hers.

Yet here I am, closing a glass door, separating us again. There's nothing to do but take everything boiling in me— the love, the loneliness, the fear for Emilia's health and safety—and pour it onto a sheet of paper embossed with the hospital's logo. There's a stack of it in a drawer along with other office supplies. I wonder how many people have conducted business in this room while waiting for a loved one to recover.

Touching the pen to the page is almost therapeutic. I can allow myself to crack open and pour out everything threatening to choke me.

Dear Emilia...

2

EMILIA

What am I doing here?

And why won't he leave me alone?

I don't know which question makes me shiver harder or makes my blood run colder. I only know I have never wrestled this kind of confusion and dread in all my life.

At least, the life I can remember.

It's easier when he's here to pretend I'm asleep. Sure, I feel sort of childish, but I would rather feel like a child than endure this guy's constant, penetrative stare. I feel it even when he's in the next room with a glass door between us. I can almost taste the expectation in his gaze. It makes me want to rip my skin off and scream until my throat bleeds.

Now I know what it means to be an animal in a cage.

Even now, I have to consciously calm myself down when panic threatens to undo me. It's a good thing they removed the heart monitor yesterday, so at least he can't hear the effect he has on me. He'd probably demand a nurse come in if he heard the beeping get faster. He's that obsessed with every aspect of my care and condition.

I don't understand it. No matter how hard I concentrate, there's no memory of him. Nothing personal or meaningful. He could very well have been the man who put me in this bed for all I know.

What do I know for sure? I know there's a constant ache in the back of my head. I know somebody hurt me badly enough to land me in the hospital and wipe out the last few months of my life—at least. I vaguely remember this past summer. I remember being assigned a partner at work, though I can't remember who it is. Mom and Dad were supposed to take their trip to Australia this autumn, weren't they? Are they still there? Would Luca know if I asked him?

Luca. Luca Santoro. The name rang a bell when I saw it on the news today, but the photo they shared of the men in the Santoro family sealed it. There was the father and his two sons—Dante, the underboss, and the younger son, Luca. Handsome, more so in person.

But dangerous.

It doesn't matter that he treats me so sweetly, like he's concerned for me. As if he'd die without me, desperate and aching, always hoping I've uncovered more of my memory. It doesn't matter that he acts like I mean something to him. Anybody can pretend. Especially a notorious criminal like him.

Either he's lying to me about us having a past, or it's something else. Was I undercover? That's the only other explanation I've been able to come up with as I lie here alone, sometimes praying for the next dose of pain meds to help me get through the worst of my headache. I hate the way they make me feel, all loopy and foggy. Still, it's better than suffering.

He told me I resigned. Is that true? Why would I? Then again, how did he know about the scar on my arm, which hasn't been visible to him thanks to the sleeves of my hospital gown? How did he know I sometimes notice numbness and tingling in my right hand? Strangely enough, his explanation brought me relief. I was starting to wonder if I was imagining the tingling, like it was all the result of my head wound. But now it makes sense, even if the implications chill me.

You would think I'd remember something so monumental, being shot and walking away from the only career I've ever wanted.

You would think I would remember being with this man.

If I could only talk to somebody I know and trust, except he won't let me have my phone. Another reason for me not to believe him. He seems caring, but how concerned can he be if he won't let me contact anybody else in my life? I could at least call the station to confirm his explanation. But no, that's something else he won't let me do, which doesn't exactly make me trust him any more than I already do, which isn't saying much since I don't trust him at all. How can I when I'm supposed to be one of the good guys, and he is most definitely not playing on my team?

Was I working on a case involving the family?

Concentrating hard only makes my head hurt worse, but that's what I need to do more than anything. I need something to focus my confused and conflicting thoughts. Rolling onto my side, I face the wall, my eyes closed quickly in case he's watching from the other room and takes consciousness as a sign I want to have a chat. That's the last thing I want or need. All he does is confuse me more than ever because if I didn't know better, I would swear there's genuine tenderness and concern in every word he utters.

My instincts are usually spot on—that much I remember. I can't believe a head injury would shake them up so badly. As far as I know, I've been here five days, and already, I'm thinking clearer, remembering more each day. Like the way I recognized Luca the day after our disastrous first meeting when all I could do was cry and feel like an alien who just landed on a strange new planet.

I need to believe more will come back in time.

What happens if I remember something horrible about him when it's already too late for me to protect myself?

What a time for the sweet scent of roses to catch my attention. Easing one eye open, I stare at the deep red blooms. They're enormous, so fragrant, and seeing them makes me smile despite knowing who they came from. He knew my favorite flower. I mean, I'm sure roses are a lot of people's favorite flowers. Still, what if he had gotten it wrong and proved he doesn't know me?

The son of a notorious mob boss wouldn't take a stupid risk.

Why would I get involved with him in the first place? It couldn't only be physical, no matter how gorgeous he is. It doesn't matter that he walks into the room and instantly commands it or that my heart tends to skip a beat when I first see him—even feeling like I do, there's no denying it. That's not enough of a reason for me to turn away from everything I ever thought I wanted and toward a man whose life is based on crime and destruction.

There's a brief knock on the door leading out to the hall, and I roll over, sitting up a little in anticipation of lunch. If there's one thing hospitals thrive on, it's sticking to schedules.

"How are we feeling?" I recognize the orderly who wears a friendly smile as he nudges the door open, tray in hand. "It feels pretty heavy. I think they doubled up your fries." He winks playfully.

"Did you tell them how much I loved the French fries?" My mouth is already watering at the thought. Hospital food is supposed to be gross, though that hasn't been my experience. I wouldn't call it gourmet or anything, but it's tasty.

"When you wouldn't stop raving about them last night?" He laughs as he places the tray on my table, which he wheels closer to the bed. "Whatever it takes to get our patients feeling better. At least, that's my opinion."

A deep, sharp voice slices its way between us. "Something you need?"

We both look toward the partly open door leading into the other side of the suite, where Luca now stands with his feet planted at shoulder-width, arms folded, and eyes blazing. It's enough to make my heart almost jump out of my chest, and I'm not the one he's glaring at.

He jerks his chin, sneering at the orderly. "Your hearing messed up?" Luca prompts when he doesn't get an answer.

"He's dropping off my lunch," I explain, though it's unnecessary. He knows damn well why this kid is in here, a kid who looks ready to pee his scrubs as he stands beside my bed. I'm glad he put the tray down before Luca decided to come in and act like a raging jackass.

Luca's mouth barely opens when he grunts out, "He dropped it off. Time to go."

I look up at the kid whose name I don't know, hoping he'll look my way so I can at least mouth the words *I'm sorry*. No such luck. He's busy gaping at the murderous man currently intent on terrifying him.

The terror deepens when Luca arches an eyebrow. "You need an escort? Move your ass." He growls, and that's enough to get the kid moving fast. It's a miracle he doesn't trip over his feet on his way out the door.

He's barely out of the room before I have to say something. Forget fear. I'm too busy being pissed. "I have an idea. Why not alienate everybody on the hospital staff?" I ask with a sigh.

Luca tips his head to the side. Can he honestly be surprised by my reaction? "Excuse me?" he asks with a snort.

"He was doing his job."

His lip curls in a sneer. "His job is to flirt with you?"

So this is how he treats women who supposedly mean the world to him. Like they're his possession. I shouldn't be surprised. "He wasn't flirting," I insist. "He was friendly and professional." *And making me glad he's around, which is something I can't imagine you ever doing.* I doubt I'd get far if I said that out loud.

Barking out a laugh, he asks, "That's what you consider professional?"

This man is insufferable. "All I'm saying is, let's maybe not make everybody afraid to come in here and take care of me. How am I supposed to get better?"

His thick lashes flutter over a pair of impossibly dark orbs, and some of the fire drains from them before his head bobs once. "Understood. I'm not trying to get in the way of your care. But I'm going to have my eyes on whoever comes in or out. That's not going to change."

And I'm supposed to love this person? Plan a future with him?

Attraction is one thing. I can imagine being attracted to him. I am now, surprisingly enough. Even with the back of my head aching with every beat of my heart, I notice the patch of tanned skin revealed by his open shirt, hinting at a broad chest and the suggestion of a tattoo occasionally peeking out when he moves. The thick arms under his sleeves, the way his slacks seem to strain around his thighs when he sits. I'm only human, and he is way too much eye candy to pretend otherwise.

But in a relationship with a brute like him? I'm almost positive this was a double cross. Like I only pretended to resign so he'd trust me and allow me into his inner circle. That means I have no idea what I can and can't say, what he does and does not know. The idea of us being any more than a detective and the man she was supposed to investigate is impossible. No matter how I try, I can't wrap my mind around it. He's a criminal, a murderer, and the complete opposite of who I try to be. I'm one of the good guys.

Aren't I? Because as much as I want to turn away from the idea, there's no ignoring it. I'm missing months of my life in which anything could have happened. I don't know who I am any more than I know the man standing in front of me now. It's horrifying, and there's no one to turn to. No one I trust and can get a hold of.

He jerks his chin toward the tray and clears his throat. "You had better eat while it's hot," he grunts out. "It smells good."

Even though it's the last thing I want, I blurt out, "Do you want some?" I lift the lid from the plate, and sure enough, a handful of French fries comes spilling off the tower somebody in the cafeteria gifted me. Why would I ask that? I don't want to spend a minute with him, much less share my food.

His lips stir in what might be the beginnings of a smile, but he shakes his head. "No, thanks. I'll be out here if you need anything." With that, he exits, returning to the sofa where he left his phone.

As I watch, munching on a fry, he picks it up, then sits

down, typing something. I wonder what it is and if I'm supposed to be documenting his actions and behaviors to report back. I doubt somebody could blame me for slacking off a little, all things considered. I won't believe I resigned until somebody confirms it for me. It would be much too convenient for him to take advantage of my condition and say whatever it is he thinks will help him. I'm not going to buy into his explanations blindly.

How the hell long is it going to take for me to get better? It needs to happen fast because I am lost in the dark, completely on my own.

It doesn't help that I can't stop watching him as I eat, admiring his sharp profile and impressive body without meaning to. I need to get better before I do something stupid, like developing a crush.

Or worse.

According to him, I've already fallen in love with him once. If that's true, I can't afford to make the same mistake again.

3

LUCA

"Remember what I said." I'm more than a little wary as I eye my sister, standing by my side in the hospital elevator. "Do not overwhelm her. She's in a fragile state."

"Sometimes I think you forget I'm eighteen and not a baby anymore," Guilia retorts, rolling eyes as dark as mine. "I get it. Don't you think I want her to get better too?"

"But you can be a little... excitable." My sister is one of the few people in the world I care enough about to go out of my way to speak kindly to. It's a short list that includes Emilia and my mother. "No throwing your arms around her, no acting upset when you see the way she looks now. That, more than anything. She's healing and will look like her old self in no time. We have to let her know she has nothing to worry about." Considering how quickly the two of them became friends, I'm hoping like hell that warm feeling will return, and Emilia will take to her again, feeling less intimidated with an ally at her side.

"I swear to God, you treat me like a child. I know how to handle myself." The way Guilia bites her lip when a soft chime tells us we've reached our floor reveals the nerves she's trying hard to hide. She's not the only one feeling a little nervous.

A long time ago, I heard something about relationships teaching us lessons. I figured it was some hippy bullshit and didn't pay much attention. Now I'm starting to wonder. Emilia has done nothing but shed light on parts of myself I would rather deny.

She's forced me to be better.

Kinder.

More patient.

Walking my sister down the hall so we can bring Emilia home tonight, I once again wrestle with doubts I'd rather pretend don't exist—about myself. how any of this will turn out, and whether I can teach her to love me again.

While I'd gladly do just about anything to be rid of the soul-crippling doubt I'm suffering, the simplest answer of walking away, washing my hands of her, is unthinkable.

I'm not giving up.

Not on us.

Rather than go straight into her room, I lead Guilia into the waiting room that's practically been my home for the past eight days. According to the doctors, it could be weeks before Emilia's symptoms fully resolve. As of my last status meeting with her team this morning, she continues to suffer occasional blurred vision and headaches that can range from irritating to debilitating. Not that she would share any of that with me.

It doesn't seem there's been much improvement in her memory of the past in the few days since she first learned who I am, and I'm not sure I should feel so relieved by that. I should only want what's best for her. But dammit, I am what's best for her.

There's no reason for her to be here any longer, though, and I can't pretend I'm not glad to be bringing her home at last, where she belongs. Having her in familiar surroundings can only help get the past back.

Emilia is sitting on her bed with a bag beside her. I brought it with me earlier today, filled with clothes for her to wear home. She waits with her hands folded in her lap, her feet slightly swinging until she sees me and instantly stills—a scared rabbit poised for flight.

Guilia releases a strained whimper when she first sees what has only been described until now, but her smile widens as we slowly approach the door between the rooms. Emilia's gaze lands on her, with nothing in her expression to give away her thoughts or whether she remembers my sister.

When I open the door, Guilia takes the lead. For once, I'm ready to stand back and let her do it rather than force my way closer to the woman I love. "You probably don't remember me," she says so softly, it's almost a whisper.

Emilia's brow furrows in concentration, and she shakes her head. "I'm sorry. I don't recognize you," she replies in a soft, sorrowful voice.

"It's okay. I'm Guilia. Luca's sister... unfortunately," she adds with a roll of her eyes that stirs Emilia's lips into a smile. "And, like, I figured you might need a little female energy in your life. We came to bring you home."

"Home? To Brooklyn?" Emilia won't look at me. The entirety of her attention is focused on Guilia, staring with an intensity that could break my heart if it wasn't already shredded after seeing her this way.

Guilia gestures toward the foot of the bed, and when Emilia nods, she perches gently on the corner. "No, not to Brooklyn."

"You live with us," I remind her from a safe distance. "I told you that already, remember?"

She remembers. She was hoping I was lying, is all. Now that Guilia is here, so sweet and sincere, she has reason to think otherwise.

Guilia reaches out to impulsively pat Emilia's leg. I can't pretend it doesn't irk the shit out of me, the fact that Emilia will allow Guilia to touch her, but not me. "I wouldn't be super happy if somebody told me I shared a house with him either," she whispers loud enough I'm sure Bruce hears her out in the hall. "But you've been with us for a while now. Maybe you'll recognize it when we get there, and we can take our walks around the compound again." There's a wistfulness in Guilia's voice that gives away her true feelings.

She's doing her damnedest to be strong and upbeat, but she misses her friend. At a time like this, when security is tighter than ever, there aren't many opportunities for distraction, which was one of the reasons why we were in the Hamptons in the first place—to give Emilia something to do and a sense of normalcy.

"I don't understand why I can't go home to my apartment," she insists, her chin trembling along with her voice.

"Because you live with me now," I tell her, though she was speaking to Guilia. "If you're ever going to get better, you have to go back to your regular life."

"Why do I have to return to someplace I don't remember? Wouldn't it make more sense for me to go someplace I *do* remember?" she asks, no, pleads.

Guilia casts a worried look my way. She can't answer this one and knows better than to try to explain. Certain things are better left in my hands. At least she's mature enough to understand that much.

"I'm going to put it to you as straight as I can," I begin.

"The people who did this to you could decide to do it again. I'm sorry to blurt it out this way, but that's where we are. I can't leave you on your own. It would be in your best interest to live on the grounds of my family's compound, where guards are on patrol around the clock. I already made the mistake of taking you off the grounds, and this was the result."

Guilia winces. "It's not your fault," she whispers, though I can't bring myself to agree, even for the sake of consoling her.

"So I'm trapped, is what you're telling me?" There's naked despair in Emilia's voice. It's like a noose around my neck that tightens with every breath I take and every silent moment between us.

"Guilia, can we have the room for a minute?" She looks up at me, her mouth open to speak, but I give her a slight head shake. This is not the time to question me. All I've managed in the hours since her release was confirmed is to count the minutes until it was time to bring her home where she belongs.

I am in no mood to be questioned or challenged. It's enough that I must bear Emilia's distrust.

Guilia excuses herself and retreats to the other half of the suite, sitting in front of the television but watching us from the corner of her eye. When I turn back to Emilia, she sits up a little straighter, always on the alert. "I know this isn't easy," I assure her softly. "I can't begin to imagine. All I want now is for you to have everything you need to get well again. I miss you." Right away, I regret the admission since all she does is recoil.

She's that disgusted by me.

We're back to where we started.

"Have I done anything to hurt you?" I ask, and it isn't

easy to sound loving when what I want is to hurl something across the room and demand she fall in line. This is the woman I love, and that's true whether or not she can remember she loves me.

I'm learning love is a double-edged sword. Only she could drive me to the brink of shattering what's left of my self-control when she's the last person who deserves it.

"Not lately," she retorts in a soft voice. "But who knows?"

I've been wounded in fights. I've been stabbed, kicked, and punched, but no physical pain could possibly compare to the anguish her dismissive question brings to life. "I love you. I know you don't remember, and I know it's not easy to believe, so I'm not asking for either of those things," I tell her.

She flinches, and her chin quivers, the only reaction she's willing to reveal. I told her I love her, and still, she needs to be stoic. "What *are* you asking for?"

"Trust. I even brought my sister with me to prove this isn't some fucked-up abduction situation. I'm not taking you somewhere to get rid of you quietly. You'll have my family with you as well. My mother has already planned a feast for you tomorrow. She loves you, too, as Guilia does. But not half as much as I do."

"I'm sorry," she offers, sounding sincere. "It's so hard to hear that when I can't remember anything about our history. I am grateful for all the care I've received here, and I'm grateful you supplied it. But..." She looks down at her hands, twisting nervously in her lap.

"Emilia. Look at me." She hesitates, eventually lifting her head until our eyes meet.

My God, she is absolutely exquisite, like a bruised flower that's somehow more striking though it's marred. Heat blazes in my chest and spreads through my body, reminding me of the countless times I've indulged in her beauty. Her sweetness and her deep, endless passion are still in there somewhere, lurking in the part of her mind that's been locked away.

Her gaze is steady, and it seems she's holding her breath as I fight my yearning body's needs. "Trust me," I urge in a soft voice. *Remember me. Love me. Accept me. Make me whole again because it would be too fucking cruel to ask me to live without you.*

Her eyes close before she winces, touching a tentative hand to the back of her head. "It hurts."

I don't know whether this is a means of changing the subject or breaking the tension that's grown between us, but I'm willing to go along if it means easing her pain. "Let's get you out of here. Once you're home, you can take a pill and go to sleep."

I hold out a hand, expecting her to place hers on top.

Shouldn't I know better by now?

Instead, she stands on her own, gripping the straps of her bag. The same bag I packed for her before taking her to the safe house after I killed the assassin my father sent to the shithole apartment she wants so badly to return to. Completely unprotected and in need of much more security measures than I could reasonably get away with without raising red flags

As if I would let her return there.

I withdraw my offered hand, fighting the burning sting of rejection. "I'll get you a wheelchair."

"I don't need a wheelchair," she grumbles, her teeth clenched like the stubborn brat she can be. "I just need a dark room and some quiet." Yet, for all her bravado, she sways once she gets on her feet. I reach out to her, supporting her thin body before it hits the floor, and my heart leaps for joy.

Here she is…

… in my arms.

Gasping, going stiff, and recoiling like my touch burns. "I'm fine. But maybe I could use a wheelchair, after all." She grunts as if the admission disappoints her, taking a seat on the bed while I go out to the hall to ask Bruce to grab a chair.

She would rather collapse on the floor than let me touch her. The thought guts me, and I need to step away before I say something I don't mean.

Being out in the hall lets me breathe easier. I'm not quite as overwhelmed as I am in her presence.

I adore this woman.

I need her like I need air.

Like blood flowing in my veins.

Yet she has no idea who I am to her or what she means to me.

It only takes the nurses a few minutes to bring a wheelchair. Then, with a half dozen guards to keep watch as they escort us, we head to the armored SUV waiting by the loading dock, where linens and other supplies are delivered. Emilia goes along with everything, not saying a word, clutching her bag to her chest like it's a shield.

I'm not naïve. I wasn't expecting a happy homecoming.

It doesn't make any of this easier.

4

EMILIA

This is the most surreal thing I've ever experienced, rolling through the gates embedded in gray stone walls, sandwiched between Luca and his sister in the back seat. A handful of flashes go off on the other side of the tinted windows, making me flinch away.

It's Luca's attempt at comfort, but his hand he briefly places on my knee makes me flinch harder. "There's been a lot of media lately," he explains in a tight voice.

Now I remember what I saw on the news about increased violence and bloodshed between his family and the other one. *What was the name again?* I can't remember, and trying to force myself to call up the memory only makes the throbbing ache in my head turn to something closer to pounding that makes my stomach churn. I don't need to make things worse.

What would those photographers think if they knew I was being driven into the compound against my will? I don't want this, *any of it.* My gut tells me Luca was telling the truth when he said this would be the safest place for me. I feel more secure now that I know it won't be just the two of us. How bizarre is that? I would rather be in a household full of murderers than be alone with one.

But they can't all be ruthless murderers. Guilia seems like a sweet girl. "Wait and see," she chirps as our driver takes us down what's closer to a boulevard than a driveway. "You'll be feeling better in no time. And when all this war stuff is cleared up, we can go shopping again at Saks."

The way she says it, it's obvious she's trying to jog my memory. When all I can do is offer a weak smile, I see the twinge of pain that etches itself in the lines over the bridge of her nose.

"Neither of you are going anywhere for the time being," Luca reminds us. I'm sure there are women in this world who would find his commanding, no-nonsense tone sexy. It makes me gag a little.

I'm sure I had to be faking my feelings for him.

As much as he irritates and repulses me, I can imagine our time together wasn't all a big sacrifice. When he keeps his mouth shut, it's easy to melt a little in the heat from his strong physical presence. His cologne is spicy and masculine, leaving me resisting the urge to lean closer and indulge in the scent.

To think it's been hours since my last dose of meds, yet I'm ready to curl up like a kitten and purr in his lap. All this because of a nice cologne and his rock-hard thigh pressed against mine. I won't stand a chance while medicated. I can only hope he gives me time and space and doesn't expect things to get physical. I could always fake my symptoms if I needed to—at least he seems respectful of that.

However, right now, I'm not faking it. When we emerge from the tall, stately trees lining both sides of the driveway, the enormous Italianate mansion in front of me is a little blurred. I try to blink it away, only the effect gets worse.

How much longer am I going to be like this? The question makes me grind my teeth against a frustrated whimper.

"What is it?" Luca looms over me, frowning with concern. Is it all pretend? I don't think so. Then again, my head is about to split open, and there are currently two of him in front of me, so what do I know?

"I'm not feeling very well," I confess. I'm sure it's obvious, anyway.

His frown deepens. Dammit, he's even handsome when he frowns. "I'll take you straight to our house," he decides. "You can always see Mama in the morning."

"She'll be so disappointed," Guilia interjects.

"Let her be disappointed," Luca growls out before one of the guards opens his door and lets a blast of cold air rush over us.

"It's all right," I insist. "I can at least say hi." Because, for one thing, I'm already tired of him deciding what I can and can't do. It's obvious he's used to getting his way and expects nothing else.

For another, the idea of us being alone together in his house makes my stomach twist into knots. I'll do whatever I can to postpone the inevitable, even with my head in a vice the way it is now.

I want more than anything to be in a dark room but not if it means having him next to me in bed. It doesn't matter how good he smells.

The house is sprawling, almost obscene, and exactly what I would expect from a mafia family. I don't remember working on a case involving them, however, anyone who's watched the local news in the past twenty years knows the name, Santoro. Here I am, about to walk into the home of the family's leader.

When Luca touches a hand to my back as we climb the

broad stone steps, I don't shrug him off. It's startling how weak I feel now. I was feeling strong at the hospital, but then I didn't do much more than cross the room. My legs are trembling by the time we reach the massive front doors flanked by two armed men, and it isn't the chill in the air that makes me shiver as we pass them on our way inside.

"Let's sit down." Luca steers me through the bright entry hall, the light from an overhead chandelier reflecting on the polished marble floors. I look around in both curiosity and wonder. So this is what blood money can buy.

The first room we reach when we've passed the sweeping staircase is soft, feminine, and full of roses. They relax me in an instant and somehow give me hope that there are actual human beings living here. Decent people, even if they do condone murder.

I need to stop thinking like this. I'll end up getting myself killed if I'm not careful.

"I'll let Mama know we're here." Guilia practically skips out of the room once Luca has me settled on a soft, deep sofa. It is such a relief to get off my feet and relax, even if there's no hope of fully relaxing with Luca hovering over me. And there I was, thinking he might give me a little space to breathe when we were back in his family home instead of the hospital—like he'd feel a little more relaxed away from hospital staff, who might make the mistake of being friendly.

"We can keep this brief," he tells me. As much as I don't want to, I hear what sounds a lot like love in his voice. Affection, at least. Intimacy.

"I don't want to be rude," I counter. How bizarre this is, trying to be polite to the wife of a mafia don. "This is a nice room," I add, leaning over a little to sniff the white roses arranged in a beautiful crystal bowl beside the sofa.

"You've been in here before," he tells me as if that's going to change things somehow.

"I don't remember anything about it. I'm sorry." Why do I feel like I should apologize? It's not like any of this is my fault. He doesn't look particularly disappointed, either.

Does he not want me to remember being here?

Did something bad happen in this room?

"Can I get you anything?" I've barely had time to process his question before he's on his feet, ready to get something for me. There's an almost frantic energy coming off him. I can imagine he's used to taking charge of things, and it's killing him to be helpless now.

"No, thank you." I might find this cute if he were anybody else. He's trying. I think he really means it. If only I could remember how I felt about him. I'm afraid to look at him for too long in case I get used to the habit of indulging in his dark eyes and razor-sharp jaw. What if I get my memory back one day, and I remember this was all part of an operation to infiltrate the family?

There are rapid footsteps in the hall before an older woman bursts into the room with her arms extended. "There she is!" she calls out, almost flying to the sofa.

Her face falls when I flinch away from her before I can help it. Her arms drop to her sides. "No, I'm sorry," I tell her right away. "My brain is moving too slowly, and I have a little headache."

"Oh, forgive me." Her voice is soft now, heavy with concern. "I should have considered that. And you must be feeling overwhelmed, I imagine."

That's a word for it. I'm almost too stunned to speak, not knowing where to look or what to pay attention to. I don't have the first damn clue of how things really are between this family and me. Who do I believe? Who do I trust?

Strangely, I want to trust her. It's the whole warm, maternal thing she has going on. In the absence of my mother, she's the next best thing. It shouldn't surprise me that I'm longing for a little maternal comfort. It's only natural I would want to believe her. Deep down inside, some part of me could remember her too. It seems like we had a nice relationship. There's nothing fake about her.

"I am a little tired," I admit. "I guess I lost some strength lying around all that time. You would think I would be rested and have energy, wouldn't you?" Why am I trying to comfort this woman? I guess it's because I sense she's kind and loving, no matter who she married or gave birth to.

"She needs to rest." Luca certainly has no problem taking the lead. He wasn't throwing his weight around in the hospital to look like a big man. He doesn't hesitate before pulling me to my feet and putting an arm around my waist like he's going to lead me somewhere, making me stiffen in distaste at his familiar attitude.

His mother's troubled expression tells me she sees the reaction his touch causes. She understands, and it makes her unhappy.

Could it be everything Luca told me was true? I really lived here. Are there people who care about me? Why? What could have changed in me to make this possible?

"Luca, *caro mio*, it could be Emilia would be better off staying alone in your house, at least for tonight." She rises and places a hand on his arm. "Especially if she is not feeling well. She needs quiet after all that time spent in the hospital." She wears a knowing smile when she turns to me, her kind eyes twinkling. "Just when you've finally begun to drift off, someone comes in to take your temperature."

I could kiss her for this. "It was frustrating," I agree,

without looking at Luca. I don't need to see the disappointment I'm sure his expression portrays.

"We will double the men at the house," she assures Luca. "Emilia needs nothing but sleep now, and she won't get that with you banging around like a bull in a China shop." I have to give it to her. She's good at handling him. She knows the right thing to say and how to say it. What might come off as an insult from anyone else is nothing but gentle, playful teasing.

Still, Luca's dark eyes are full of regret and doubt when I finally get the nerve to meet his gaze. What did he think was going to happen? Was I supposed to beg him to take me home so we could be alone together?

"Triple the men," he eventually grunts out. "And I am here if you need anything. Your phone is down at the house. My number is programmed in it."

My phone. There I was, thinking I might never get it back. If he was hoping to score a little credit for keeping his word, I don't mind giving it to him. "Thank you. That means a lot."

"I'll walk you down." He's almost able to hold back a groan when I hesitate but not quite. "You have nothing to worry about. There's something I need to discuss with you, that's all." It's clear he's annoyed, at the very least. I'm not giving him what he wants, like falling into his arms or something.

"We'll see you tomorrow, only if you're feeling up to it." His mother takes my hand and pats it gently before Luca leads me from the room. "We'll have a big dinner for you."

"Thank you so much." I sort of hate to leave her, not to mention Guilia. But her instincts were spot on. I need to be alone. My headache feels slightly better, and the blurred vision is no longer there, but who knows how long it will last.

Two armed men follow us out of the house and down the steps. "Take your time," Luca urges. "Don't tire yourself out."

"I'll be okay." I'm not so sharp with him anymore. How can I be when he is so protective? It's a little annoying, yet I'm starting to believe it comes from a good place.

"What is it you want to talk about?" I ask as we walk down a gravel path to a smaller house than the one we left, but one too big to be called a tiny dwelling or however they're referred to. It's definitely newer than the main home, with gray stone and oversized windows spread out over a single floor.

"Like I said, your phone is waiting for you inside," he reminds me. "There's something you need to know. You hadn't yet told your parents about us. We were going to work out a plan for that together, you and I, while we were on vacation. We never got the chance."

It makes sense. No matter my reasons for being with Luca, it's not like I could tell my parents without things getting very tricky and fast. I'm having a hard time believing I ever had anything to do with him. It would be ten times worse for my parents, especially Mom.

"They should be back soon from their trip," I offer, mentally crossing my fingers. "Where were they going again?" I whisper, pretending I don't remember.

He jumps straight in. "It was supposed to be a tour of the Outback. Three months, if I remember correctly."

He's right. They spent a year planning that trip, anticipating and bringing it up at every opportunity. No way I could've forgotten that. And he knew about it. Another bit of proof.

"But they came back already," he continues. "You didn't know how to tell them. On top of that, there was your resignation."

Reaching the house, Luca comes to a stop before turning to me. Solar lights cast a glow across his finely chiseled features. Between that and the moonlight, a girl could swoon. Of course, that could also be the exhaustion threatening to take my legs out from under me.

"They don't know about that, either," he explains with a sigh. "I thought you should know before you reach out to your mom or dad."

"I guess this is another secret I'll be keeping for a while." I run a hand over my head, shuddering at what I feel. I've never been vain and have been known to go months without a trim, too busy, distracted by work. I still feel like a monster, thanks to the stitches running along my scalp.

"We'll figure something out. You don't have to go through this on your own." He takes half a step closer, and I find myself trembling. Is it fear or anticipation that makes goose bumps pebble across my skin?

For one second, a flash of desire explodes deep in my belly. It's almost enough to make me strain upward, standing on my toes to meet his lips with mine.

In other words, I need to lie down.

Alone.

"Hopefully, I'll be able to think better once I've slept," I murmur, wrapping my arms around myself and blowing out a shaky breath that turns to vapor.

His brows draw together, eyes narrowed dangerously, and there's a second where my chest tightens until my air is cut off before he heaves a sigh. "Right. Come on. Let's get you inside," he grunts out, clearly offended.

Two guards flank the front door, both nodding in silent

greeting as Luca unlocks the door and opens it, ushering me inside. This is no humble little cottage. It's luxurious, full of furniture, electronics, and appliances I wouldn't dream of having in my apartment if I could afford them.

He moves quickly, walking through the living room and past the open kitchen until he reaches the doorway through which I see the bed. "Bathroom's in here," he tells me, flipping a switch to turn on the lights. "I'm going to grab a few things to take up to the house."

Meanwhile, I can't take my attention off the king-size bed. I've slept in this bed. My skin tingles against my will at the thought of rolling around in the sheets, my body locked with the body of the man now moving around the room. That's something I wish I could remember. I mean, if I degraded myself by associating with a mobster, I hope the sex was good.

I have a hard time believing it could be anything but, especially when our eyes meet across the room and a flash of heat races through me. "Thank you for everything," I whisper for lack of anything better to say. It isn't easy to get my thoughts together when I'm this aroused.

"Whatever it takes to get you well again." There's something sweet in that simple wish, even if he delivers it awkwardly. "You're going to get well. You'll be your old self again."

I wonder which of us he's trying to convince.

He hesitates, stalling for time, before finally leaving me on my own. Well, not exactly. The house will be surrounded by men all night. When Luca's gone, it's like a weight has lifted off me—the pressure of trying to compose myself and put on a brave face in the middle of so much confusion. Right away, I grab my phone from the nightstand. It's off but plugged into a charger. Once powered up, I find a dozen missed texts from Mom, along with a handful of calls she made over the past few days.

Mom: *Can't wait for our dinner.*

Sent three days ago.

When I didn't reply, she started getting antsy and making calls. The last text I sent her talks about having dinner together after I return from vacation. So that part of Luca's story is true, as well. We went away together. I was planning on meeting with my parents afterward.

In other words, he's telling me the truth. I don't know whether that's a comfort or not. I've completely lost sight of who I am any more, and the more I think about it, the worse my head hurts.

After stripping down to my underwear, I find one of my oversized T-shirts in the dresser and pull it on. *I really lived here.* Why, dammit? I'm no closer to understanding by the time I pull back the comforter and slide under. The bed is worlds beyond what I slept on in the hospital, and immediately, my tired muscles begin to relax.

Tomorrow, I'll do more digging around if I feel up to it and maybe see if I can bring back any memories.

The sooner I get them back, the better.

5

LUCA

A hand landing heavily on my shoulder jars me awake. I didn't realize I had drifted off to sleep. "Sorry," Niccolo grunts out, backing away with his hands in the air. "I didn't know you were asleep."

"Neither did I." I sit up straighter on the leather sofa and look around my father's study. We're the only two people here. "I thought we were having a meeting."

My cousin looks up and down. "We are. Have you been waiting here long?"

A glance at my phone tells me I haven't. It hasn't been more than a few minutes since I came in and sat. That was all it took for me to fall asleep and start dreaming. What a relief Nico came in when he did because it was a familiar nightmare I would rather not repeat—sprinting down that fluorescent-lit hall, passing one identical door after another before reaching the room where Emilia was left. Sometimes, the hall never ends, and I can't get her, no matter how hard I run. Other times, I find her, but it's too late. She's already gone.

Nico watches me, puzzled and a little concerned. "Tell

me you got some sleep last night, man. She's back, she's safe." He drops beside me before trying to stifle a yawn and failing.

"She's not safe until he's out of the picture," I snap.

He groans before scrubbing his hands over his face. "We're doing everything we can. I know it's taking too long."

"Too fucking long. Don't get me wrong. I know you're looking under every rock to find that son of a bitch." I nudge him with my elbow and jerk my chin when he looks my way. "He's vermin, and vermin know how to hide."

Shuffling footfalls accompany my father's appearance. At least one of us looks like he slept last night. He managed to shave, too, unlike me. "I understand everything went according to plan," Papa begins, not bothering with the formalities of a greeting.

"Everything went fine," I assure him. "Not so much as a hint of trouble." Aside from the fact that I can barely touch my woman without her recoiling. Not to mention a night spent fighting the urge to go down to the house and at least sleep on the sofa. Anything, so long as it means being closer to her.

"I understand she'll stay on her own at the house." My father eyes me warily as he lowers himself into the chair behind the desk. "She is on the same page as you when it comes to what she can and can't share with others?"

Dante's voice rings out behind me before I have a chance to reply. "I don't think she should have her phone yet," he reminds us.

"So fucking original, Dante," I snap, folding my arms and turning to face my brother.

"Careful." He tucks his phone into his pocket before mimicking my stance.

"What's this bullshit?" Papa waves a hand back and forth

between us. "You were behaving yourselves for a while there. Do me a favor and don't start with this childish fuckery again. We have business to discuss before we call the cop." He rarely refers to Craig by his first name. Dirty cop or not, he's currently our best chance at finding Alessandro and ending his miserable life.

"How are Paul and Rob doing?" I ask my father, referring to two of the men who were critically injured during a shootout with a group of Vitali associates. They crossed paths outside a restaurant in Hell's Kitchen, and the next thing you know, they landed both families in the past week's news cycle.

He groans before rubbing his temples. "Dante?"

Dante blows out a sigh. "Paul is still comatose, and the doctors are starting to talk about doing those tests they run to see if a person's brain is firing anymore."

"Christ," Nico mutters.

"But Rob seems like he'll pull through," Dante continues. "He lost his spleen, and he's always going to walk with a limp thanks to a bullet he took to the femur, but he got lucky. Not like Chris and Marco." There's regret in his voice, even if the idiots brought it on themselves if it's true they fired first.

"Stupid, headstrong punks," Papa mutters. "The hell did they think they were doing? Starting shit out in public, civilians all around, not to mention all the blowback. Like we needed the family's name in the news for days on end."

He snaps his fingers, signaling for Dante to pay attention. "I want arrangements sent to the funerals on behalf of the family. And send something to Paul's mother. She was always a nice lady. Our mamas were good friends. There was a time they imagined making a match with us, joining our families." He snorts softly, his gaze unfocused before he swivels in his chair to gaze out the window.

Fuck me. I shoot a look at my brother, and for once, he seems to notice what I've known for a while. There's something wrong with Papa. He's not who he used to be. He wouldn't trail off in the middle of a meeting and lose track of himself. No fucking way. This, on top of his worsening fatigue and the collapse he suffered one day a few weeks ago, I'm more certain than ever he's hiding something from us.

Dante clears his throat loudly, and I do the same. Nico coughs behind his clenched fist.

That stirs Papa, who turns around and scowls when he finds the three of us watching him. "Where's Francesco?" he demands before checking his watch.

Something has to be said. We can't pretend there's nothing unusual going on here. "Papa, are you all right?" I ask, sitting in the chair next to Dante's.

Papa's head snaps back, and a familiar look of derision twists his mouth. "I had a little difficulty on the toilet this morning... nothing a bit of fiber won't cure. Would you like the fucking details, son?"

At least that sounds like the man I know. He seems to have gone from weariness straight through to resentment. It reminds me of my grandfather's decline. I was just a kid, maybe seven or eight years old, but I remember him being angry all the time over the last few months of his life and resentful of anyone who offered to help him. Men like us don't want to be pitied or worried over.

"As for Francesco, he hasn't yet come back from combing through one of the Vitali-owned whorehouses out in the Bronx, looking for Alessandro. He checked in with me, though. He'll be back soon." Dante checks the time and scowls. "He won't make the call with Craig, but he doesn't need to be here. Speaking of which, let's get it rolling."

Craig blurts out a question the moment the call connects, his voice filtering through the speaker and filling the room with anxious energy. "How is Emilia?"

Papa frowns, then looks guilty when he meets my gaze. "She's fine," he grunts out. He might have warmed up to the idea of her living here, but that doesn't mean he wants to waste time discussing her condition. There are limits, and we have bigger problems on our hands. I have to accept that.

Dante glances at Papa before speaking. "We need news. What do you have?"

Craig's heavy sigh tells an entire story before he says a word. "The closest thing I have to intel hints at him hiding out with some woman he supports. He could be in Jersey somewhere," he reports flatly.

"Pussy," I mutter.

Imagine that. Hiding behind a woman after leaving another woman for dead. He must have assumed she was, or at least that it wouldn't take long given her state. Why else would he take the chance of leaving her there?

"You know we're doing everything we can. He took it way too far." Craig's voice breaks a little before he clears his throat. "We're going to find him."

"How the fuck did Alessandro know we were in the Hamptons?" I look around the room and am met by equally blank expressions. They don't know any better than I do, and it's gone beyond the point of chapping my ass to consider Vitali having the upper hand.

"It could be you were followed out there," Craig reasons. "Or one of the guys you took with you could've been working with the Vitali crew and were killed to keep them silent."

"No way," Dante grunts out while the rest of us shake our heads. We know our men. Papa pays them almost too much, all to keep them loyal.

"At any rate, I'm doing everything I can," Craig tells us. "I would like to come by and see her. Who knows? I might help bring her memory back."

Papa shakes his head. "Soon, maybe, but not yet. We've got these fucking photographers hanging around, watching to see who comes and goes. Once things quiet down, maybe then. We can't risk a cop being spotted."

With a resigned sigh, Craig replies, "Understood. I'll keep you posted." I'm glad for the opportunity to end the meeting when he ends the call. I've already spent too much time away from my reason for living.

"I'm going down to the house to check on her." Either nobody sees fit to stop me, or they know better than to try. The house might as well be on fire, I'm walking so fast, barely short of jogging.

I need her.

I'm a fish out of water without her, gasping for air.

On my way outside, I cross paths with my cousin, Francesco. He's bleary-eyed and clearly annoyed. "That motherfucker is a ghost," he snarls out, gulping from a cardboard cup of what smells like strong coffee. "I need to scrub off my top layer skin after combing through those so-called establishments he runs."

For the second time this morning, there's an unspoken apology nestled in an unrequested explanation. "I know you're doing all you can," I assure him before moving on. Frankly, I don't have the time or the patience right now to go through the same song and dance I went through with Nico. Not when she's down there waiting for me.

Only she isn't waiting, and I know it. She likely dreads

my return. There is no ignoring the fear creasing the corners of her eyes whenever I draw too close. And it isn't like it was when she first crashed into my life. There's no excitement in knowing I unnerve her. Because now, I love her and know the thrill of being loved by her.

Like the old song says, the thrill is gone. I refuse to believe it's gone forever. What we have is too strong and powerful, something neither of us could fight against. Something so strong, even my family couldn't break it.

I open the door without bothering to knock. The living room and kitchen are exactly as I left them last night, untouched. There isn't so much as a dent in the throw pillows to tell me she's strayed from the bedroom since I left.

My heart clenches when I hear an instantly identifiable sound coming from the bathroom. Some sounds are like that. As soon as you hear them, the entire story is clear. In this case, Emilia's almost violent vomiting hints at the misery she must be going through.

"It's me," I call out as I approach the bedroom, then venture close to the partly open bathroom door.

"Don't come in." Her weak, pained voice leaves me reaching for the door, anyway. I ease it open far enough to see her kneeling in front of the bowl, her arms wrapped around it, her body trembling pitifully.

"Let me help you." I don't know how. Caregiving has never been on my list of skills. Another aspect of myself she's revealed, whether I like it or not.

"Disgusting..." She gags again, but nothing comes up. I return to the kitchen, grab water from the refrigerator, and open the bottle on my way back to her. She flushes the toilet and lowers the lid before resting her forehead against it.

"Are you strong enough to stand?" She weakly grunts before I drape her arm over my neck and help her to her feet. She swishes a mouthful of water and spits it into the sink before leaning against me, letting me lead her back to bed.

Looking at the nightstand in the light coming in from the bathroom, I ask, "Where are your meds? When was the last time you took one?"

"I haven't..." She half groans, half whimpers, her head hanging low. The room goes completely dark as soon as I turn off the bathroom light, blackout curtains drawn tight.

"I was there when the doctor talked to you about pain management. You have to be proactive, remember? Before it gets to be too much." Everything she brought from the hospital is in her bag, which I find at the foot of the bed. The bottle of pills is on top, and I'm almost annoyed with her for leaving it there.

I soften when she whimpers again. "Here," I murmur more softly this time, holding out one of the tablets. She doesn't hesitate before taking it, gulping down more water.

"Empty stomach," she whispers as she eases herself into lying down. She moves so slowly, carefully, like she's afraid she'll break otherwise.

"Here's hoping you can sleep and the nausea won't bother you too badly." I've done almost all I can, and she's still in pain. What do I do now? How do I help her? The doctors said this could continue for a while until she finishes healing, and unless a severe headache lasts more than a full day or comes along with slurred speech or loss of coordination, it's nothing to be alarmed about.

Easy for them to fucking say. They don't have to stand by and watch their reason for existence suffering the way she is now. She doesn't deserve this. If only it were as easy as deciding to absorb someone else's pain. I would take hers in a heartbeat.

She doesn't react when her phone buzzes on the nightstand. It's a call from her mother. I pick up the phone, intending to send the call to voicemail so as not to disturb her. When I do, an alert on the screen tells me this is one of five missed calls. I can't imagine Emilia not checking her phone last night the second she was alone, which means these calls have all come in since then. Otherwise, there would probably be many more listed.

I'm about to return the phone to the table when low and behold, the screen lights up again with another call from Mom. Emilia only groans softly, her back to me. While I'm watching her, what I see in my mind is a belligerent woman raising shit because she can't get a hold of her daughter. I can't risk her making noise, going down to Emilia's old station and demanding somebody put her in touch with a girl who no longer works there anymore.

I don't want to do it, but it seems like the only viable option. Stepping out of the bedroom, I close the door behind me before answering the call. "This is Emilia's phone. Emilia is all right," I quickly add before she gets any ideas. "But she's too sick to talk. Is this Mrs. Washington?"

There's a moment of silence before a woman answers. "Yes. Where is my daughter? Who are you? What do you mean, she's feeling sick? I want to talk to her." Fear rings out in her voice, more intense with every word.

"She has a bad headache and isn't in great shape. A migraine, I'm guessing." A harmless lie. There's no way I can tell her the truth. I wouldn't know where to begin. Emilia might only end up hating me worse if I tried.

"And who are you?" she demands.

"I'm..." *I almost got her killed. I love her more than life itself, and she doesn't even know who the fuck I am anymore.* "I'm a good friend of hers. I'm sure she'll get back to you once the headache clears up." When all I get in return is silence, I add, "I understand we're all supposed to get together for dinner sometime soon. I'm looking forward to it."

It's like a lightbulb finally goes on. "Oh! That kind of friend! Emilia didn't tell me!" There I was, hoping to prove I know her daughter and only want to take care of her, but she sounds like she wants to start planning the wedding.

"Then let's pretend I didn't say anything since she might get annoyed with me for telling you." Her soft laugh tells me I'm charming enough to disarm her. It's a farce, beginning to end, yet it's working. She's happy to believe me since I sound intelligent, charming, and kind. That's the kind of man she wants for her daughter.

It's a relief to end the call and drop the act. Now, as I ask myself what to do next to help Emilia, I have her demanding mother on my mind along with everything else. I can only hope I haven't complicated the situation further.

6

EMILIA

I died.

I died and went to hell.

I'm being tortured for every bad thing I've ever done as I lie here in the darkness, afraid to move. It hurts so much worse when I do. But then it hurts when I don't, driving me to try to turn my head this way and that, hoping it will help. It has to. I can't take much more of this. It's like my brain is being torn to pieces inside my skull.

I need to relax, an impossible task thanks to the panic that keeps wanting to wipe out everything else. Panic that the pain will never stop, and I'm going to feel this way forever. It's childish and stupid. I know this will end. There's no comforting myself with that when all I know, all that's real, is pain. Agony.

I barely hear the bedroom door open and close again. *Luca.* I don't have it in me to be afraid or put off by his presence. I can't think about him right now, not when I'm like this.

"What can I do for you?" he whispers, and it surprises me to find how close he came on silent feet. He is already on the other side of the bed, in front of me, leaning close enough that his breath hits my face.

"Nothing," I whisper, and that is a struggle in and of itself. "It hurts so much."

"It usually takes around twenty to thirty minutes for the medication to start taking effect." I should accept what he's telling me without question. I mean, there are much bigger problems going on, such as how I'm going to live through this moment.

"Oh God, are you sure?" I beg him to be right as I count down the seconds in my head to get my mind off the pain.

"I asked the doctor," he explains. He's gentle, but his voice is something close to laughter. The bed shifts, telling me he's sitting down. "Of course, I wanted to know everything I could about how to take care of you as soon as we got home."

Strange. The sweet simplicity in his explanation is enough to bring me as close to a smile as I can manage. For the first time in hours, I can think about something other than the pain. "Thank you," I whisper. There's more I could express, but I can't muster the strength.

"You don't have to thank me. It's what I do when it comes to you," he tells me lovingly. There's more movement, and I realize he's stretched out next to me. I should recoil. I should push him away. I don't have the strength to do either, and right now, I don't want to. Not when I'm the closest I've come to feeling comfortable since the pain woke me up a few hours after I fell asleep.

It was stupid to avoid the pills. Stubborn. It was the fear of how weak and foggy they'd make me that kept me from taking one. "This is so bad," I admit, holding myself very still for fear of what will happen if I move, expecting the sharp lance of pain to slice through me again.

"And I am so sorry you have to go through it. Hold on." Suddenly, he's off the bed, and I hear him in the bathroom before he returns. "Mama used to do this for me when I was little. Maybe it will help."

The touch of a cool washcloth against my forehead is a surprise at first, but the sensation is nice. "Feels good." I sigh.

"Focus on that," he softly croons. "Think about how good it feels."

"Tell me something?" I ask as he strokes my forehead.

"Anything. What do you want to know?" With my eyes closed, I can almost pretend he's somebody else. Someone I should be with—an honest, decent man.

"No, I mean, tell me a story," I whisper. "Something to distract me."

"Distract you? Hmm..." He shifts a little, and soon, his voice comes from very close to me, face-to-face, only inches apart. I still can't bring myself to open my eyes, but I feel him. "You kicked my ass in poker when we first got to know each other. More than once."

"I did? I am a pretty good poker player."

"No shit," he grumbles, lacking any animosity. "I was convinced I was getting hustled. How did you get to be so good?"

"When I was in the academy, a group of guys would get together for a weekly game. I learned how to play so I could join them."

"Why did you do that?" he asks.

"I wanted to fit in." Laughing is the last thing I should feel like doing, yet I have to snicker at myself. "All I ended up doing was annoying them when I beat them."

He chuckles warmly. "Sounds about right. You put everything you have into everything you do."

"I try."

"Did you notice all the little things you've placed around the house? Did you have time to look around?" I grunt that I haven't. "There are some pictures of you and your parents, books, and knickknacks you brought from your apartment. Before you came here, I lived in this house, but it didn't feel like a home. It was my refuge, a way to be on my own. But it wasn't home until you showed up. I would come down from meetings up at the house and open the door, and it would smell like food and your perfume. Sometimes, you'd be playing music and dancing as you chopped or stirred. And it felt so right. I didn't know it was missing until you came along."

I'm overwhelmed. The emotion in his voice and the affection and intimacy are too much to handle. I would cry if I didn't know damn well how much worse the pain would get. This man genuinely cares for me. He actually loves me. I've added something to his life and can't imagine why or how.

"I never had much of an excuse to cook for just myself," I admit. "I'm sure it's nice to have an excuse to do it."

"I like your meatballs better than Mama's," he confesses in a loud whisper. "She would clutch her pearls and faint if she ever heard me say that."

"Your secret is safe with me," I promise, and we laugh softly. The medication is starting to work its magic, and the tangled knot of pounding agony at the back of my head starts to loosen. I can almost believe it won't last forever.

"We weren't supposed to fall in love, you know." He speaks slowly, still stroking my forehead with the cloth now and then, letting it run down my temple and over my jaw. "I guess you would have figured that out by now."

"I've been wondering," I murmur. A deep breath eases

the pain a little further, then another after that. Finally, I can think again.

"We couldn't help it. At least, I know I couldn't. I met you one night at the club I run," he explains. "You spilled your wine on my jacket, and I was a goner the second you looked up at me. Your eyes took my breath away. And your body?"

I'm not imagining the soft growl that follows, just as I'm not imagining the sizzle of pleasure that runs up my spine at the sound of it. Yes, I can believe an instant attraction flaring up between us because, even now, when I feel like death warmed over, part of me wants to be closer to him, like my body remembers what my brain can't. The way we fit together, the way we work.

I'm craving it.

I need it.

We don't always get what we need, do we? Now is not the time. There might never be a time for all I know, but if the time exists, it most definitely is not right now.

I'm starting to feel a little hazy, losing my grip on myself. I welcome the sensation. It is much nicer than the agony so intense it makes me want to die.

"So that's how we met," I whisper. "I was wondering." I must've known who he was, right? Why would I have walked into his club? I don't party. I never have, always throwing myself into work. I must have been there to investigate him. Either I'm on an undercover assignment, or I was no stronger against the pull he has on me than I am now. Eventually, I succumbed.

I wasn't confident enough to tell my parents, was I? Something was holding me back. Here I am, with no memory of any of it, and my parents are going to want answers. I wish I had gotten it out of the way before I was injured, but we can't predict things like this.

"I have never, ever regretted that night or anything between us that came after." His voice is so deep and rich, like warm honey poured over me. My body lights up, heating, and I realize my headache is gone. It may as well have never existed. All I know now is I want to curl up in his arms. I want to be held, touched, cherished.

It has to be the drugs. I need to be stronger than this. So he has his moments where he's not a complete and total monster, even though I can't erase the harm I'm sure he's done. No matter how kind he can be, he is not a good person. No matter how piercing his eyes are, the way his muscles clench under his tight shirt, or how much my body wants his.

It's not the washcloth touching my skin anymore. It's the back of his fingers, his knuckles grazing my cheek where bruises are finally healing. "Sleep. You need sleep more than anything. We both do, I think." I wish he'd keep talking. His voice is like a sonata carrying me on one gentle note after another.

Before long, the sound fades away like it's coming from the other end of a long tunnel. I want to ask if he's going to sleep, too, but there's no time before true darkness closes in around me and wipes everything away.

7

LUCA

The mood around the room is fucking grim as my father finishes a phone call from my cousin, Francesco. "We'll have to make an appearance at the funeral," he tells Cesco, who went to the hospital to check on Paul's condition. The doctors were supposed to test him today to see whether he had brain function. Suffice it to say he no longer does, and any organs that can be used will be harvested and donated.

"I don't know if anyone from the family would be welcome there." Cesco's voice is tight, strained. "After his mother fainted and came to, she screamed a lot about how it was all the family's fault. How she never wanted him to get involved the way his old man was and how she knew he would end up dead before he was twenty-six like her husband did."

"Jesus Christ." Papa closes his eyes, and a look of pain touches his weathered face. "So much for having a long history with somebody."

"It's to be expected," Dante muses, pacing back and forth in front of Papa's desk. "She's emotional. She just found out her only son is dead. She's hurting. Nobody told him to pull a gun." I can't tell whether he believes that or if he's trying to reassure Papa he's not responsible for a kid's death. And Paul wasn't the only one.

"I'll be heading back soon," Cesco concludes.

"Nobody can say we abandoned the kid in his final moments," Papa reminds us after ending the call. He sounds sad but resolute. "Let's settle up the bill with the hospital. Whatever she thinks about the family, she shouldn't have to pay it. The kid wasn't even old enough to be married or have a family, was he?"

Nothing can be said about that, so we remain silent, the three of us lost in our heads. However, my mind is only focused on one thing these days.

Falling asleep next to Emilia yesterday was exactly what I needed. Fully clothed except for my shoes, on top of the covers, I slept like the dead for a solid seven hours and woke up groggy and confused in the middle of the afternoon. Emilia kept sleeping, and I was glad to let her do it. I brought her soup and fresh bread, which she ate in bed while I distracted myself with the television in the living room.

Yes, I wanted to be with her. Yes, it fucking killed me to give her the space she needs. But it felt like a step in the right direction, and it gives me hope that we'll pull out of this together. The fact that she was able to fall asleep with me in bed alongside her is another minor miracle. She's coming around—slowly, yes, but it's happening. There's no stopping it. She's going to remember she is mine if it fucking kills me.

And when she does, I intend to spend days celebrating that, preferably in bed.

We break for lunch after discussing business that, for

once, has nothing to do with the name Vitali. It's easy to lose sight of what remains to be done to keep the family running. I've always had difficulty focusing on things that don't interest me—probably one of the main reasons why my brother would be better suited to run the family, besides the fact he's the older son. There's never been a challenge like the one I'm up against now when nothing in the world is as critical to my existence as my love.

Dante rambles on about shipments while I wonder about Emilia. Is she well today? Guilia was supposed to take breakfast down to her this morning to check in on her. I've been with Papa all morning and haven't gotten a report yet. I suppose if there were an emergency, I would've heard about it by now. However, that does nothing to ease my worries.

By the time my brother is finished, I'm already beyond the point of losing my patience. I'm going to go down and see her. I need to know for myself that she's okay. We're breaking for lunch, anyway, before I have to sit down with the club's books for a while.

I'm barely a dozen strides from the office when somebody calls out my name. "Luca! Where are you headed?" I turn to my sister's voice and find her grinning like a Cheshire cat as she approaches on mile-high heels that click against the floor with every step.

"Where do you think?" I ask, raising an eyebrow. She looks bright and cheerful in a furry miniskirt and somehow manages to walk without breaking her neck. "I should ask you that question. Where do you think you're going in that get-up?" I ask, folding my arms, temporarily distracted.

She rolls her heavily made-up eyes. "What difference does it make? I'm only wearing it around here since there's nowhere to go." She looks down at herself and sighs softly. "I mean, I'm wasting all this on you people."

"What's the alternative?" I only purse my lips disapprovingly because I know it gets under her skin. "Driving some poor bastard out of his mind? Teasing every man who lays eyes on you?"

"Oh God, would you shut up?" She hisses while her cheeks color. "That's just exactly the kind of thing I don't need Papa to hear, for fuck's sake."

"I'm just saying. Don't let him catch you like that, no matter whether you're staying around the house or not." Guilia has long been one of the few patches of brightness in our lives. She's the only girl and spoiled to hell and back, but she is a good kid with a beautiful heart. All the more reason to distrust every man on Earth since I know all too well how men think.

I'm about to walk away when she stops me, scurrying in front of me and placing her hands against my chest. "Hold on. There's a surprise for you."

"No offense, but I'm not in the mood for surprises." I love the kid, although sometimes she has trouble taking a hint.

Her eyes twinkle despite my growing irritation. "Are you sure about that? Because I think you'll like this one." She practically skips off down the hall, heading toward the dining room. Once I've finished wondering how the hell she managed to skip in those shoes, I follow, curiosity getting the better of me.

"Ta-da!" My sister steps aside as soon as we enter the room, beaming as she waves her arms with a dramatic flourish. Emilia is sitting down at the table with Mama and having tea.

I'm a moth drawn to a flame, moving toward her before I've had time to think. "How are you feeling?" I ask as my eyes crawl over her, taking in every aspect of her down to the shy smile she offers.

Mama rises, arms outstretched. "Isn't it nice?" she gushes after kissing both my cheeks. "We convinced her to join us for lunch today."

"And I'm glad you did," Emilia tells her before looking my way again. "I'm feeling better, thanks."

I can't take my eyes off her. She has a little bit of lost weight to make up for, and the sweater she's wearing hangs on her. It doesn't help that she pulls her hands into the sleeves and hunches her shoulders protectively when I touch one of them. "It's nice being able to sit and talk," she says as I take a seat beside her. "I'm trying to get my brain moving. Sitting alone isn't going to help that."

"How are you really feeling?" I ask in a quieter voice, my stomach growling once I've settled in. I had no desire to eat until this very minute. Knowing she's all right has left room for other concerns to be addressed. I have to be better about that. I can't fail her by losing track of myself. What good could I do if she needs protection and I'm too exhausted to be of any use?

"A little shaky," she murmurs with a brave yet weak smile while Mama argues gently with Guilia over her taste in clothes. "But better, for sure."

"That's a relief." What isn't a relief is the way she continues to keep herself away from me, sitting straight and tall when she used to lean in like she couldn't be without my touch for long. I don't know how much longer I'll be able to stand it. She needs all of my patience and devotion now, though. I can't let her down, no matter how much I want to overturn this entire fucking table.

"We have chicken cacciatore and pasta for lunch," Mama informs us. "And a big salad. I hope you're hungry."

She eyes Emilia with concern, something only I seem to notice.

She pats Emilia's arm. "We need to put some meat back on those bones, *cara mia*. You're going to disappear before my very eyes."

"You're so thoughtful." I can tell she's feeling over-whelmed but doing her best to cover it. It's the way she fidgets, fingers picking at the tablecloth where only I can see. "I feel so bad not being able to remember you."

"Oh, you don't need to feel any guilt." My mother takes her hands and holds them tight. There's almost feverish intensity in her gaze as she stares at Emilia. "You must never apologize for that. It's not your fault. All you have to do is take care of yourself now. We are all here for you."

"Maybe it's not all bad, her memory being lost." Only I heard my sister's soft whisper, and my head snaps around so I can glare at her.

"The hell are you talking about?" I demand as quietly as I can.

"I'm just saying she would never have come up to the house otherwise. She was always afraid of Dante." Guilia's big eyes are full of fear as she gulps. "I'm sorry. I didn't mean anything by it."

"Don't pay any attention to me," I tell her, shaking my head at myself. "Look, I'm on the edge. Okay, sis?"

"Well! How nice." I know my father well enough to recognize the effort he's making at sounding pleasant and cheerful when he finds Emilia seated at his table. "It's good to see you up and around." He shows no surprise or shock at her condition, which has gone unseen by him until now. He's kind enough to keep his reaction muted.

"Mr. Santoro, I have to thank you." Emilia starts to rise,

but he shakes his head before taking his customary seat at the opposite end of the table from where Mama sits.

"You have nothing to thank me for," he tells her, flashing a brief smile. "We are all happy you're back with us." Part of me believes him, but I'm not kidding myself. If he's happy, it's for my sake. She's been a thorn in his side from the start.

As always, Dante enters the room on our father's heels like the little dog he is. We might have come to a tentative understanding while Emilia was missing, and I am grateful for all the work he put into trying to locate her and the continuing work he's doing to pin Alessandro down. That's not enough to wash away the bad taste that always fills my mouth when I see my brother trailing behind Papa, practically touching his lips to the man's ass. It's pathetic, though of course, he doesn't see it that way. I doubt he's ever been honest enough with himself to recognize his pitiful ass-kissing for what it is.

He doesn't say a word. He doesn't have to. The scowl he wears tells me what he's thinking. The prick. At least he's smart enough to keep his mouth shut, something he doesn't always do.

When Papa's eyes bulge, my heart lodges itself in my throat. For the first time today, Emilia isn't the only thing on my mind. "What's the matter?" I'm already halfway out of my chair with my heart in my throat, prepared to call the doctor if need be when I finally notice what he's staring at to generate this reaction.

"What the hell do you think you're wearing?" he growls out at Guilia, who made the mistake of getting out of her chair to kiss him on the cheek. He wouldn't have noticed if she had stayed in her chair—rookie mistake.

She steps back and looks down at herself, chewing her

lip. "I just wanted to dress up a little. That's all." Her voice is small and full of apologies.

"Dress up?" he bellows. "You're hardly dressed in the first place. No daughter of mine is going to walk around looking like a *puttana* so long as I'm the head of this family." Poor Guilia flinches at his ugly language, and I hear Emilia's sympathetic groan at my side.

"*Mio amore*," Mama murmurs, clicking her tongue. "Do not upset yourself." I notice she doesn't defend Guilia. She knows better. It's a safer tactic, urging him not to upset himself rather than asking him to ease up on the poor kid.

"I encouraged her to buy that skirt," Emilia blurts out, much to my surprise. She's usually too intimidated to say much in front of Papa, although she doesn't remember how things started out here. The fact that he was seriously considering having her killed to the point where he hired an assassin, then put her life up to a vote after I foiled his plans. "I thought it looked nice on her. It's my fault."

Guilia's mouth falls open as she slowly turns toward Emilia. "You remember that?" she asks, wide-eyed in awe.

Fuck me, she's right. My chest fills with warmth and leaves me breathless as I ask, "You remember?" I can't believe how much is riding on a simple memory.

Her mouth drops open the way Guilia's did. "I do... I think," she amends, chewing her lip. "We went to Saks, and I bought... a black dress, right?"

"Yes! You did!" My heart is soaring as I pull her into a hug without thinking. She's coming back to me.

I knew she would.

She has to.

What's even better is the way she melts into my embrace. "It came to me out of nowhere," she says with a shaky laugh and emotion clogging her voice. "I didn't hardly think about it. It was just there."

She's still laughing as she pulls back a little, beaming brightly, her blue eyes sparkling as they stare into mine. It's like nothing's changed. The warmth is there, the familiarity.

The love.

Until I lean in, drawn to her, ready to kiss her waiting lips.

Her eyelids flutter before she goes stiff and wiggles out of my embrace. As quickly as it soared, my heart drops, and I'm reminded of the way things are. No matter how desperately I need her to remember, I can't force it. As far as she's concerned, I'm nobody to her. A stranger she might have known but can't quite place.

I'm barely able to clench my jaw and grind my teeth in time to hold back a scream of pure anguish. Frustration. Even rage. She's here, next to me, close enough to touch and smell, but it doesn't matter.

And there's a chance it never will. It's too painful to think she may never know what we had together.

Past tense.

No, we aren't a thing of the past. I just need to be patient.

The only thing I can do is force a smile for the sake of the women in the room rather than hurling something through the window, the way everything in me demands I do. I swallow my disappointment back rather than taking her by the shoulders and shaking her hard, screaming into her face, demanding she remember me. All that will do is cause her more pain. Not show her my love. Our love. Everything we sacrificed for each other now feels like a waste if it ends with her hating me for who I am.

8

EMILIA

That was awkward and almost scary.

I should be thrilled. Over the moon. Relieved that I remembered something as small as a shopping trip. It should give me hope and strength. I should be celebrating because, for the first time in days, it feels like there's a reason to celebrate.

So why am I so goddamn miserable as I sit here alone in this beautiful, unfamiliar house?

It was obvious Luca was glad to see me go from the main house. He didn't try to convince me to stick around or offer to walk me down here. He was relieved, and I think I know why. I'm sorry for it and not trying to hurt him, no matter what he's done or how many people he's hurt—or worse.

I have to give him credit. There was clear, blazing anger sizzling through him after that pivotal moment when it was clear he wanted to kiss me, and I stopped him before he had the chance. I turned him down. Rejected him. He was enraged by that and maybe embarrassed since it happened in front of his family. I'm not sure whether any of them noticed. I hope they didn't, and not only for his sake. He doesn't strike me as a guy who lets go of grudges easily.

He has this dangerous edge to him.

That's not even the worst part.

I wish it was.

A sick chill runs through me and leaves me reaching for a throw pillow on the sofa, where I'm sitting in front of the television, paying no attention to the movie I switched on when I got here—anything to fill the silence. The pillow provides no comfort, no matter how tightly I clutch it.

I wanted him to kiss me.

I wanted to kiss him.

For a split second, it felt inevitable. An inhale following an exhale. The sort of thing you do without thinking, like a habit. He leaned in, and I was going to lean in to meet his mouth with mine. I wanted nothing more than to melt into his arms.

I wanted him to hold me.

I wanted him to do a lot more than that, in fact. An hour later, I can almost feel the furious buzzing that exploded in my core and radiated outward. The heavy veil hanging between us lifted for that split second and revealed something that might still exist deep down in my consciousness.

And I don't know how to feel about it.

How to feel about me.

I should not want him.

I can't want him.

Yet I do.

It sickens me.

I sicken me.

My heart lurches when my cell rings, though it startles me out of my self-loathing for a moment. Normally, I'd be glad to get a call from Mom at a time like this. I'm feeling about as low as I ever have, questioning everything about myself and what might have led me to this place.

It's not like I can tell her anything about what's going on. I should answer, though. I've kept her waiting long enough. I'll have to fumble my way through it. And who knows? I might hear her voice and remember something important.

"Will wonders never cease?" she asks when I answer the phone. "I was starting to think I would never hear your voice again! Are you feeling better?"

She's ever the pro when it comes to bombarding me with questions. Some things haven't changed. It would be comforting if I weren't so completely confused. "Feeling better?" I question. *What a weird thing to say.*

"Your friend told me you had a migraine when I called yesterday. I must've called six or seven times before he finally answered," she informs me accusingly.

It's like the floor shifts with her admission, leaving me fighting to keep my footing. "Oh. I didn't know he answered. I must've been asleep," I murmur. Do I sound like myself? I can't let her know there's a problem when I don't have the first clue how I'd explain the situation.

"Who is he?" It's obvious she's been driving herself nuts since their conversation, dying to find out about him. I can almost see her pacing the house, wondering why I never told her about him, salivating as she anticipated this inter-rogation.

And here I am, wondering why he didn't tell me he spoke with her. It might have been nice to get a heads-up.

"A friend." She used that word, right? "He's a friend of mine."

"A friend who said he knew we were planning on having dinner together... whoops," she adds with a light giggle. "I wasn't supposed to mention that, though he said he's looking forward to it. He sounds very cute, sweetheart. I want details." Her voice practically drips with excitement.

Now, I wholeheartedly wish he had told me about their little chat. This is like one of those dreams where you find yourself in a final exam for a class you didn't attend all semester. Only it's genuine. "There isn't very much to tell. You'll meet him when we have dinner." I could kill him for putting me on the spot like this.

"What's his name?" she demands. It's amazing how suddenly she switches from excitement to brittle irritation. "I don't like this whole secretive thing you have going on lately. First, you can't tell me what you're doing at work. You make it sound like you're on some undercover mission or whatever it's called."

I did? Maybe I was. I figured it had to be something like that, right?

"Then... you tell me you're going away and we'll get together when you're back. Only you vanish off the face of the Earth for two weeks without a hint of your plans or even a quick text to let me know you're still alive. You know your father and I have had our reservations in the past over your work and how much time you devote to it. I'm starting to think it's becoming a real problem, Emilia." Finally, she stops to take a breath after her tirade.

Laughing would be the worst possible reaction, which is the only reason I'm able to contain myself. Imagine complaining about me working too hard when, according to Luca, I no longer have a job. Or do I? Was I telling the truth about my undercover work? I find it hard to believe I would ever confide something like that, but I don't know the first damn thing anymore. What's harder to believe? Would I admit to an undercover assignment or fall in love with a mob man?

"Honey?" Mom's voice is noticeably softer after several silent moments pass. "Are you there? I didn't mean to upset you. I worry, is all, and you aren't helping things by avoiding me."

As it turns out, a head injury isn't enough to help me avoid feeling like a terrible, negligent daughter. "I'm sorry," I mumble, falling back against the sofa cushions with the throw pillow still clutched tight to my chest. "It's all been so complicated. And I'm still feeling wrung-out and shaky after the migraine."

"You didn't sound so wrung out until this very second, young lady, so don't think you're going to hand me an excuse." Of all times for her to pull the angry mom act on me, refusing to accept a weak excuse for the sake of keeping the peace.

My jaw is starting to ache from grinding my teeth. "I'm serious. I don't feel well, and this isn't helping." It isn't a lie, either. There's a storm building in my head, one fueled by my mother's incessant bitching and confusion over whether this whole thing with Luca was real or not. Closing my eyes doesn't help. Neither does taking slow, deep breaths to calm my blood pressure before it soars to the point of no return.

"I haven't felt well in weeks, thanks to my daughter treating me like a stranger," she retorts. "We're going to dinner this Saturday night. No excuses, no talking your way out of it. Your father will make a reservation at Luigi's for the four of us."

Her announcement makes me sit straight up. "I have a better idea. Luca will make the reservation for Saturday night." Because I have no idea where we'll be safe if there's any such place in existence. "He's, like, that sort of guy. I'm sure he'll want to pay for everything too. Warn Dad in advance."

She snickers, and I can tell she's starting to come around a little. "That's all we need. The two of them arguing over the check and causing a scene."

I don't want to underestimate him, but I would put nothing past somebody who looked like he wanted to kill me for refusing his kiss earlier. What a fun little surprise Dad would get if Luca pulled a gun. "It'll be nice," I tell her, though I fear it will be anything but.

Saturday. That's four days from now. What do I do if my memory is still gone? How do I get through it?

"We're looking forward to meeting him," she tells me with excitement in her voice. "Now, don't think you can get away with conveniently forgetting to tell me where we're having dinner. We'll set up a tent outside your front door if that's what it takes. You are not going to avoid us forever."

No. God forbid. "Don't worry. I'll let you know as soon as Luca makes the reservation. I'd better go take something for my head before it gets bad again." Before ending the call, I add, "I love you."

I can barely wait long enough to make sure the call is disconnected before throwing the phone to the floor, then pressing the pillow to my face and screaming my heart out. All the confusion, the dread, the frustration. The loneliness. Fear.

By the time my voice gives out, I'm empty and weak. Not weak enough to stop the tears flowing freely down my cheeks. What am I doing here? What do I believe? Who can I trust? I've always been able to rely on myself. How do I navigate this when I'm the least reliable person in this entire fucked-up situation?

I'm curled in a ball, lying on the sofa and weeping when the front door opens without warning. It's bizarre, the brief flash of relief at the sight of Luca as he steps into the house.

It dies a quick death, especially when I remind myself he's a big part of why I'm in this terrible, confusing place in my life.

He knows nothing of this. He only sees me crying, and it brings him to his knees beside the sofa. "What is it?" he whispers in that soft, warm, intimate voice that I wish didn't touch some hidden part of me that craves it.

No. I crave comfort and safety. That does not mean I crave Luca Santoro.

"What is it?" I echo and sit up, throwing the pillow aside and making him grunt in surprise. "Let's see. I don't know who to believe. I don't know who I am, why I can't go home, and why I didn't just say to hell with it and confess every-thing to my mom so I can go back to my old life, goddammit!"

Something darkens his eyes until they look nearly black. "You were on the phone with your mother?" he asks, only it sounds like he's confirming I stole his wallet or murdered his dog.

I blink hard in disbelief. "That's what you took from everything I said? Yes, I was on the phone. Sorry if that hurts your plan in some way."

"What the hell are you talking about?" He barks out a humorless laugh. "My plan? What plan is that?"

His derision only intensifies my outrage, turning my blood to lava. "Your plan to keep me all to yourself," I snap. "You're cutting me off from the entire world. You can't blame me for not trusting you because of that. I just... I just..." My lungs can't pull in enough air for me to continue. *I just want to go home. I just want to remember my life. I want everything to go back to normal.*

I want it not to feel so right when Luca enfolds me in his arms and pulls me close after I burst into tears again. A part of me demands I push him away, but right now, that voice is small, far beneath the surface. The rest of me wants very much to be held and comforted, even if it means by him.

"All I want is to keep you safe," he insists, murmuring into my ear while I weep on his shoulder, wondering which of us I hate more. "That's all. I'm here for you. Let me be here for you."

Sadly, I want to let him. It's because I'm lonely, confused, and scared of the unknown that I lean into his embrace, my arms snaking around his neck so I can hold on tight. Like I'll fly away if there's nothing keeping me on the ground.

Something takes over. Instinct, maybe. Something that makes it possible to turn my face toward his neck or inhale his spicy cologne and the unique scent of his skin. It stirs something in me— memory? Or am I so hard up for comfort that being this close to him feels like a good thing?

He pulls back far enough to look into my eyes. "Let me protect you," he whispers, undoing me a little bit at a time with every word that tumbles from his generous mouth. "Let me love you. It's all I ever want to do. That's all I ask."

It can't be.

I can't allow it.

No matter how right it feels when his gaze lowers to my lips, revealing his thoughts. No matter how easy it is for me to close my eyes the instant after he leans in, almost lunging, like he can't wait another second before crushing his lips to mine. The instant our mouths touch, an explosion erupts in my core. Shock waves roll through me, sending sizzles of pleasure radiating from head to toe. I'm alive. I'm really alive, and something close to joy replaces all the pain and the fear as the kiss deepens, his tongue stroking mine, his arms tightening possessively.

And I love it.

Deep down, so deep there's no room for a conscious thought, I love this. I want it. I want *him.* My fingers run through his thick, silky hair until he growls into my mouth, his hands running up and down my back. All at once, I want to take off my clothes so he can touch my skin. So he can mark it and make me his.

This is why I have no choice but to shove him away as hard as I can before I make the sort of mistake there's no coming back from. It doesn't matter that he somehow reaches some deep, dark part of me I didn't know existed. My aching nipples and throbbing pussy don't mean a thing. I'm not an animal.

I have a choice.

He is not my choice.

"No," I gasp, fighting for breath. "No, Luca. It's not going to be that easy."

9

LUCA

Fuck this.

I'm fighting a raging hard-on as I stand, glaring down at her. What more do I have to do? Who does she need me to be? "You need to make up your mind," I growl out and immediately regret my tone. I can't help it. It's fucking exhausting being the supportive, loving partner who is uncertain if the love of his life will ever come back. "That, or you need to stop getting in your own damn way," I add, lowering my voice.

"Exactly how am I doing that?" She jumps to her feet, her blue eyes flashing, her tits rising and falling with every ragged breath. "What, because I won't let myself do something I know isn't right?" she adds with steely determination.

"Isn't right? Look around," I reply, this time louder, \ her head snaps back, and her brow furrows at the volume of my voice.

I'm fighting a battle with myself to give her time. The not knowing that has me teetering on the edge. If I knew she'd come back to me, I would be more patient. I'd wait forever.

"Look." I grab a framed photo off the end table and thrust it toward her. "Your parents, pretending they're holding up the Leaning Tower of Pisa. Look, another one." This time, it's a graduation photo with Emilia in the center wearing a cap and gown and her parents standing on either side. "You lived here. This was becoming your home too."

I shove the photo into her hands, then turn toward the bookshelves. "Look at all of this. Do you think I'm a big fan of the *Harry Potter* books? Because you sure as hell seem to be." I run a finger along the spines of the thick books. "What, do you think these belong to me? Then there's your things in the bathroom. Your clothes in the bedroom! What more do I have to do to prove to you I'm not making this shit up, Emilia?"

She's always had the power to uncover the best and worst in me, prying up rocks and revealing what's squirming underneath. It shouldn't thrill and satisfy me to watch her fade in the wake of my rage, but then I haven't had much satisfaction lately.

"Stop yelling at me," she yells back. "You don't have the right."

"Yes, I fucking well do," I shout, weighted with guilt. "Because I have done *everything* I can to make you feel comfortable, show you this is where you belong, and that we belong together. What is it going to take?"

"I'm so sorry I can't get my memory back on your goddamn schedule!" Her chin quivers, but she holds her head high. Part of me rejoices at the sight. She's still in there somewhere. The woman I fell in love with against all odds, even common sense.

What about the part of her that fell in love with me? Is that still there? Will it ever return?

All the old instincts come rushing back. The way things

were between us in the beginning. "Why don't you stop lying to yourself?" I ask, crossing the room one slow, measured step at a time. My hands tighten into fists as I imagine throwing her over my shoulder, carrying her to the bed, and reminding her who she's dealing with. Her mind might not remember me, but her body does.

She gulps, backing up until her legs hit the sofa. "What point do you think you're making?" She's not so feisty now. Damn me to hell. My dick twitches when I identify the fear that's begun to creep across her face. I thought I was beyond the point where intimidating her turned me on, but I used to think a lot of things that have turned out to be untrue. I believed we were safe and unbreakable, and look where it got me.

"You think I didn't feel the way your body reacted to me?" I murmur, eyes tethered to her, my pleasure growing with every short breath she takes. Her dread is getting worse by the moment. More than that, she lowers her gaze and folds her arms because she knows I'm right.

She's too embarrassed to look me in the eye. "Don't act like you know me," she whispers fiercely, struggling to hold onto any shred of dignity and self-possession she can muster.

"But I do," I tell her, advancing slowly like a predator cornering its prey. "That's the thing. I know you inside out, my love."

The problem with refusing to look at me is her inability to judge when I'm too close for her to escape. Her sharp gasp rings out when I take hold of her hips and pull her against me in one quick movement.

This is how it's supposed to be. Fuck being gentle with her, giving her time and space. She belongs to me, and I now know part of her remembers that. We've never been able to deny our physical connection. It was part of what brought us together in the first place.

"Stop fighting it," I growl out, breathing in her sweet, enticing scent. It's more intense now that her heart is hammering, every flutter of her pulse sending a fresh burst of her essence into the air. I would love nothing more than to close my eyes and soak it in, to take the rest of the day to reacquaint myself with her after holding myself back all this time. "You have no idea how much I want you. There's no way you don't want me."

"I don't." It's a whimper, a whine, something a stubborn child would say when fighting off their bedtime. Pointless, a waste of energy, yet she insists on denying herself what she needs.

Digging my fingers into her supple flesh, I growl again, the animal in me ready to attack. "I have kissed, licked, stroked every inch of your body," I whisper, my lips no more than a hair's breadth from her ear. She shivers, and it's a small victory that pushes me onward. "You've done the same to mine. Your body remembers the feeling of having me inside you."

"Luca," she breathes out weakly, her teeth grazing her bottom lip. I told her she didn't have a chance against me, but then she always has to learn the hard way.

"Some things can't be denied," I tell her, my hands sliding around until they're cupping her ass. No matter how hard she bites her lip, there's no containing a helpless moan. "This is what I should have done in the first place. I should've known it would be the quickest way to get through to you because it's the part of you that can't be denied. You fought like hell against it, and you lost the fight." My teeth graze her earlobe, tugging a little before I kiss it softly.

She shudders with a dismayed little groan, not a second before doing what I knew she'd do all along. She turns her face toward mine, seeking my kiss.

And I give it to her, covering her mouth, claiming it again.

Mine.

All fucking mine.

My heart is pounding out of my chest by the time I pick her up, holding her close to me as I carry her across the room. I don't stop until we reach the bed, where I lower her without breaking our kiss and stretch out on top of her delicate body.

Her fingers have curled into something closer to claws, raking across my shoulders before sliding down my back to tug my shirt from my waistband. My blood is humming, racing. An urgency like I've never known overwhelms my every thought and movement. I know what I've missed these long, lonely days, and this is the answer to every prayer I never dared voice.

Her touch is the sweetest fire. It singes me, burning. I'll never heal. I don't want to. She's already branded my soul. She may as well do the same to my body. My skin seems to sizzle as her fingers dance up and down my bare back, bunching the shirt around my shoulders. Every deep moan that tumbles from her luscious lips makes my dick twitch in anticipation.

I want to take my time, indulge in everything we've been unable to share for too long, but the way her pussy grinds against my rigid length tells me this might be over soon. I need the feeling of her wrapped around me, drawing me deeper, milking me.

"So fucking hot," I groan out against her skin, cupping her covered tit and rubbing it before she yanks up her sweater to give me access to more of her. This is the Emilia I've missed—greedy, hungry, and unafraid to show it.

Burying my face between her tits, I lap at her skin, running my tongue under the cups. "Oh God," she moans out, rewarding me by grinding harder against my dick.

Her enjoyment only makes me more determined to pleasure her. She's been through so much, and I want to take her away from it and reintroduce her to everything we're capable of together. "Yes..." she rasps out when I pull on one of the cups to reveal her taut nipple and flick it with my tongue. Her fingers run through my hair before tugging hard while she moans. "Yes, Luca."

When she stiffens with no warning, I let out a disbelieving laugh. She already came? We've barely done anything.

Yet when I lift my head and look down at her, prepared to tease her a little, the shock printed on her flushed face freezes my blood. "What is it?" I ask, forgetting everything. "Did I hurt you somehow?"

Her eyelids flutter before she releases a shuddering breath. "I saw something... in my head. Oh God, get off me!" She's twice as desperate now to get away from me as she was to have me all over her. When I don't move fast enough, she wiggles out from underneath me and scrambles off the bed, putting her clothes in place before wrapping our arms around her trembling body.

"What was it?" I sit up, confused, breathless, and aching like hell. I'm so hard I might break my zipper, but that seems like the last thing on her mind as she starts pacing tight circles beside the bed.

"My eyes were closed just now," she whispers, staring at the floor. She may as well be talking to herself. "And I saw a dark, dirty room. I was on this filthy little cot, and there were these men... these men who..."

She comes to a dead stop and covers her head with her hands. "And they did this. I was afraid to move." Her voice rises in pitch until it's almost a squeak that pierces my chest. "I was afraid they would slice me up."

Shaking, she turns to me, her eyes bulging. "What the fuck happened to me? Why did you tell me I was attacked?"

She's slipping through my fingers, pulling further away no matter how tightly I try to hold on. "You were," I insist. "That's what you were remembering. Your attack."

It's when I stand, prepared to hold her and comfort her, that she backs away. "No. That's not the full story. Now I get it." She laughs, high-pitched, almost hysterical. "It wasn't just that somebody hurt me, and they might want to hurt me again. It didn't have anything to do with my job, either. It was you," she snarls out, her teeth bared.

"No!" I insist. "I would never—"

"Stop! That's not what I meant. And don't touch me," she snaps when I reach out to do just that. "I was... I was abducted, wasn't I? They held me in that dark room. It wasn't just like some guys grabbing me and beating me up in an alley to send you a message." Her voice shakes and rises in pitch as more of it comes back. "Somebody took me out of a house. I was alone. I was fighting... I remember fighting... something about my shoe? Oh, dammit, I don't know!"

Her hand claws at her temple as she tries to piece it all together. She's teetering on the edge, about to fall apart. Holding her together is more important than defending myself. "You have to sit down," I urge. "Breathe. You need to calm down before you give yourself a headache."

She slaps my hand away when I reach out again and

touch her shoulder. "Don't tell me what I need." Her lip curls in disgust when, moments ago, she was kissing me and moaning my name. "What else haven't you told me? What else am I going to have to find out on my own?"

"If you would stop being hysterical for a minute, we could—"

"What a great idea!" She throws back her head and laughs. "Tell the woman you supposedly love that she's being hysterical."

"Shitty choice of words," I admit, and it's taking everything I have in me to keep myself in check for her sake. There's a roaring in my head to go with the pounding in my chest. I don't need this. Not her anger or outrage, or the blame, especially not the blame, which I've heaped on myself all this time.

"What are you going to tell me now?" she demands. "What nice story are you going to give me? What excuse? Maybe you can bring your mother down to soften me this time."

"Don't do that." I shake my head, leveling a stern gaze her way. That was a low blow. "Please don't bring my mother into this," I grit out, trying my hardest not to lose my shit again.

She blinks rapidly before swallowing. "No. You're right. She actually seems like a nice person. Guilia, too," she adds. "I wish I could say the same for everyone else. But all I get from you is half-truths or no truth at all," she snaps before her eyes light up. "Why didn't you tell me you talked to my mom yesterday?"

I can barely keep up with how her thoughts bounce from one to the other. "I didn't get around to it."

She throws her hands into the air with another laugh. "Congratulations. You put me in another shitty position. But

I'll tell you right now..." she insists with an edge to her voice, "... you are not coming to dinner to meet my family. Forget it. I'm not playing pretend for anybody."

"You think it's that easy?" When she spins on her heel to leave the bedroom, I beat her to the door, blocking the way. "You are not going anywhere alone, so don't entertain the idea. I'm coming with you, and there will be guards watching us, and that's final. Because whether you like it or not, there's still danger out there."

"Thanks to *you,*" she reminds me, eyes narrowed, her voice more like a snake's hiss.

It's nothing worse than what I've told myself countless times, yet much more potent coming from her mouth. "Yes. Thanks to me. And you fucking knew there was danger, and you wanted to be with me, anyway. So what does that say about your high-and-mighty ass?"

Her eyes widen like she's in pain and something shocked her hard enough to make her rock back on her heels. One painfully silent moment after another passes with neither of us doing anything except breathing and staring at each other.

"I have to get out of here," she says in a breathless rush, looking around for her shoes, which she shoves her feet into. She's frantic, shaking, eager to get away from me. The person who loves her more than anyone ever has or will.

I don't sound loving when I demand, "Where do you think you're going?"

"On a walk. Don't worry," she adds with a bitter laugh over her shoulder. "I wouldn't dream of leaving my cage."

"Emilia, please just stay and talk—"

"I've heard enough lies for now. Thanks very much." She shoves her way past me, and I don't bother stopping her because if she doesn't get out of my sight, this will get a lot uglier than it already has. The small bit of sense remaining in my overheated brain knows this is only going to get worse. I'm only making things worse when all I want to do is make everything right between us. She pulls on her coat and leaves without another word, slamming the door hard enough to make the windows rattle.

I reach for the closest thing to me, which happens to be another photo of her parents. The satisfaction of hurling it across the room is short-lived, nothing but a memory by the time the broken frame hits the floor.

Broken the way we are.

I have to wonder if there's any way to put us back together.

10

EMILIA

I should say something, shouldn't I?

Sitting in the back seat of this car, my hand resting on the box I picked up minutes ago at the wig maker's shop in the shopping village. Luca sits on the box's other side, involved with his phone.

Aside from making the arrangements for a last-minute appointment at the shop, we haven't said much to each other since that disaster a few days ago. I still cringe when I think about it. I was so ready, practically on the verge of begging him to fuck me, when those ugly memories came back.

I wish I understood why. Why then? It's like being tortured, plain and simple. I was about to have what was bound to be the best sex of my entire life, and then bam! Traumatic memories came slamming through the door and shoved all thoughts of sex aside. I went from floating in bliss to drowning in fear, unable to process the nasty images crashing into my head and the intense emotions they stirred up. I still can't quite process it.

When things cooled off, and it was clear there was no

getting out of this dinner tonight, it was time to start thinking logically. One thing was obvious. I couldn't go to dinner with my parents looking the way I do. As it is, a knit hat is the only thing making it possible for me to show my face in public.

It's one thing to practically have a crew cut, but the stitches along the back of my scalp are plainly visible, thanks to my lack of hair.

"Thank you for going to the trouble," I murmur, staring at my hand rather than looking at Luca. "Arranging for all of this, you know. I appreciate it."

He grunts at first, his thumbs moving over the screen. After another few moments, he mutters, "They're supposed to be the best. The most natural-looking. You feel good having it on?"

Good isn't the word. Once the living, breathing angel at the shop showed me how to put on the wig and what I would need to do to style it, I was able to look at myself in the mirror. I could've cried. For the first time in forever, I felt like myself. I looked like me, not some shadow of who I used to be.

"It looks great," I tell him.

"I'm glad," he retorts with a humorless snort before going back to his phone. "I went through enough trouble getting you in at the last minute."

What a charmer. Every little jewel that falls from his lips makes me wonder how I or anyone else could fall in love with a man like him. I'm supposed to act like everything is fine and dandy during this dinner when just the act of sitting this close to him makes my skin crawl.

Right. Keep telling yourself that.

Okay, so he doesn't always have that effect on me. Even now, with the temperature between us downright icy, I find myself squeezing my thighs together in memory of the mind-blowing reaction I had to him. I was on fire, barely in control of myself. I hardly recognized the person I had become, but that wasn't enough to stop me. Only the memory that bubbled up was strong enough, probably because my mind was free of questions and worries for the first time in ages. Who can think when they're in the middle of trying to rip somebody's clothes off?

I need him to be on his best behavior tonight, and the grumpy lump-of-shit act he's pulling right now isn't going to fly. I need to find some way to mend fences. "You said we've been to this restaurant before? The one we're going to tonight?"

Watching him out of the corner of my eye, I notice the typing stops. "Yes. I bought out the place for the night. You wanted a normal experience, and things weren't safe enough for us to go out without taking extra precautions."

I wish I could remember that. Something nice, something good. Even if I were faking my feelings, it would be a memory to cling to now, when we have to play the happy couple for my parents or risk all kinds of ugliness I don't want to imagine.

It's going to get ugly either way. Dad will recognize him. He's a chronic news watcher. Considering he raised me to be the kind of person who would never associate with criminals, he's going to be shocked, to put it mildly. I'll be lucky if we get out of this without a public fight.

No, that's not Dad's style. He would much rather walk out. Either way, it's going to be humiliating.

"Nervous?" I turn my head at Luca's sudden question, and he glances at my fingers, tapping rapidly against the top of the box.

"A little," I admit. "I don't want this to turn into a thing.

You know, if I thought there was any way we could get out of it, I would." I'm trying to be nice and smooth things over, but he only scowls.

"Of course you would," he mutters with a bitter snort. "You would rather do anything than have people think you would debase yourself by being involved with me." I can't help but notice a sadness underneath all that bravado.

The thing is, he's right, though he doesn't need to throw it in my face. It isn't my fault he chooses to live the way he does.

"You fucking knew there was danger, and you wanted to be with me, anyway. So what does that say about your high-and-mighty ass?" That nasty question hurled at me in rage has echoed in my head ever since. Could it be true? Could I have been with him despite the danger? Was this real for me?

Staring out the window, I watch the city go by in a blur. It's midafternoon, and the sidewalks are clogged with people bundled up against icy winds that bring the smell of snow with them. I used to be part of all of that. I was a normal person with a normal life.

"What was my partner's name again?" I ask since I was too overwhelmed to commit it to memory when I first asked back in the hospital.

He looks up at me, arching an eyebrow. "Craig. Do you remember anything about him?"

"Only that he exists. I can't picture his face in my head." Why does it sound like this amuses him?

"Spoiler... he was working for us all along." When I can't hide my surprise, he snickers. "You're not a big fan of his. He's been asking about you, though. Wanting to know if he can come and say hi, maybe jog your memory."

"Why would I want to see him?" I ask out in disgust. A dirty cop. Then again, I guess I'm no better since I was supposedly in a relationship with this man and went as far as moving in with him. But Craig could give me a little insight into what I was doing when I met Luca. Or would he only lie to me because he's on the family's payroll?

Every time I answer a question, three more questions pop up.

That's what is still on my mind hours later as I finish getting ready for a dinner I've been dreading. Makeup helps cover the thin, pink line on my cheek where somebody hit me hard enough to split the skin. I can almost remember that—the pain, the sudden shock. It's like having a name on the tip of my tongue, and the harder I try to remember, the further away it gets.

I need to stop trying. That's the problem. That's why I remembered what I did when I was in bed with Luca. But do I want to? That's the thing. What a shame we can't decide what we want to take with us and what can dissolve into the ether.

I carefully pull on the wig and adjust it the way the woman did at the shop. The blonde waves cascade past my shoulders and look extremely natural. I toss them back and forth, a little giddy at finally having hair again.

"Are you almost ready?" I hear Luca before he enters the bedroom to find me standing in front of the mirror spanning the length of the dresser. He stops short, and I watch his reflection as he takes in the sight of me. "You're beautiful," he declares.

For the first time, there's no lust or longing in that simple statement. He says it like it's a simple fact. Somebody should tell him that's a much more effective tactic at warming me up a little. "Thank you. And thank you again for this." I run a hand over my new locks, grinning.

"I would do anything for you." He clears his throat and

straightens his blue necktie before straightening the lapels of his charcoal suit jacket.

Luca is drop-dead gorgeous, especially wearing a suit that was obviously made for him. Everything about him exudes wealth and confidence.

I wish there wasn't that little voice inside me, warning me against staring for too long. A strange sense of yearning stirs in my chest, and I almost wish I could be who he needs me to be.

He's a killer, you idiot—a fact I can't afford to forget.

Once we're in the car, I text Mom to let her know we're on our way. "I hope neither of them notice the guards," I murmur, one of so many concerns I have for tonight.

"It's their job to fade into the background." I wish I could feel as confident as he sounds. Something tells me tables full of men dining together in what's supposed to be an intimate, even romantic restaurant might stick out a little.

I hope they're good at their jobs, or else we might be screwed. My parents included.

I'm probably overthinking things, reacting out of dread.

I glance his way to find him staring at my legs. He doesn't bother looking away when I notice. "You remember the story we're telling?" I prompt, snapping my fingers when he doesn't answer or acknowledge me.

"Do I remember?" he asks with a smirk. "I gave it to you. And it's the truth." But is it the full truth? I don't know. I won't until my memory returns.

My heart is thudding as we approach the restaurant. A couple of guys are hanging around near the front door, and I wonder if they're Luca's men. It's freezing outside, and I have to remind myself that it's their job before I feel sorry for them.

The cold takes my breath away as Luca helps me out of

the car, or maybe it's the touch of his hand. There's no denying the physical pull he has on me. It's strong enough that I could easily see myself straining upward for a kiss once we're standing face-to-face—or almost, thanks to my heels. It almost feels natural.

Almost. My fears stop me yet again, and I pull back. "Ready?" I whisper, ignoring his brief frown.

"And if I said no?" Yet he walks me to the door, an arm around my waist, the image of a perfect gentleman as he escorts me inside to the hostess stand. Anyone would believe we're a happy couple.

"There you are!" I barely have a chance to turn at the sound of my mother's voice before she has thrown her arms around me, squeezing tight. "I was starting to worry you would never show."

The familiar scent of her signature Pleasures perfume is enough to make my heart swell and leaves me fighting back emotion. Once she lets go only enough to hold me at arm's length, I note, "We're on time. Didn't you get my text telling you we were on the way?"

Her familiar blue eyes roll. "Sure, but you still could've come up with some excuse to keep from seeing us." She looks me up and down and offers an approving smile. "You look nice. Maybe a little too thin, but that's always been true."

"Mind if I get a chance to say hello to my daughter?" Dad has always been the calming influence, the one who smooths Mom's sharp edges. A hug from him is like coming home, and I am unwilling to let go right away. I'm myself now. I know who I am.

That is until I hear Mom behind us. "And you must be Luca." Her voice has obvious approval, and I don't doubt she's reacting to his good looks. Who wouldn't?

"I am, Mrs. Washington. It's a pleasure. I see where Emilia's beauty originates." He knows how to turn on the charm when he has to, and his voice practically drips with it before she giggles like a teenager.

Dad's pleasant smile fades as he studies Luca over the top of my head. *No, no, please. Don't cause a scene.* "Have we met before?" he asks as they shake hands.

"I don't think so, sir." Luca leaves it there before taking my hand. I squeeze his as hard as I can, but he doesn't react, cool and calm. I guess deception comes more naturally to him.

The hostess waves us on, and we follow her lead, passing one table after another. I even recognize a couple of the guys scattered around the dining room, having seen them outside the house on occasion. Luca was right. They do blend in.

Dad is no closer to being convinced by the time we sit at a table near the back of the room. I notice the way Luca positions himself with his back to the wall so he can see everything. What would it be like, always having to look over my shoulder?

"You look very familiar to me," Dad murmurs just as he takes his seat across from Luca.

"Do you have any pictures from your trip?" I ask, raising my voice until it's a little louder than his. "I've been dying to see them."

"Oh, yes, I have them on my phone." Mom pulls it out and opens her photo app. "You really should go, honey. You would love it."

"That's what you say after all your trips," I point out. It feels good to remember something like that, something normal. And I'm glad for the photos since they'll provide a distraction.

I don't feel like devolving into awkward small talk that can't lead anywhere good.

"Do you travel much, Luca?" Mom asks as I scroll through one photo after another.

"I would like to," he tells her. "I'm usually too busy with work to consider it."

"And what is it you do for a living?" she asks while I die inside.

Dammit. I can't keep myself from cringing at the question. I look at Luca from the corner of my eye, holding my breath. "I help run my family business," he explains smoothly. "I generally do whatever my father asks. We have business interests throughout the city."

"Business. That's interesting." Mom leans over to look at the photos I'm pulling up. "Oh, that was a terrific day. We saw—"

"Business?" Dad's voice is flat, tight. The way he sounds when he's suspicious and following a hunch. "What kind of business?"

"What is this?" Mom asks with a light laugh. "An interrogation? Honey, that's enough." All I can do is hope that, with all my might, he will listen to her.

He doesn't. "I know who you are. I know your face." My blood runs cold, and my body stiffens as my father's head swings slowly in my direction so he can stare at me in horror. "What is this all about? What are you doing with this man?"

Well, there goes that. We haven't even ordered appetizers, and already the night is ruined. "Dad, don't," I whisper. "Please."

"Will someone please clue me in?" Mom's gaze swings back and forth over the table.

"Maybe I can explain," Luca offers. He reminds me of his

father right now, wearing the same stern expression Rocco does when he sits at the head of the family table. "My name is Luca Santoro."

Mom gasps with her usual dramatic flair before staring wide-eyed at me. "Santoro? *Those* Santoros?"

"Those Santoros," Luca murmurs evenly, a wry grin playing over his mouth. I'm glad he finds this amusing while I sit here trying not to throw up. "I know this must come as a shock."

"That's why I didn't really want to tell you any specifics," I murmur, chewing my lip as I watch them process all of this. Doing it in public was a mistake, but it's too late now. "I knew you would think the worst. I was trying to find a way to explain."

"And have you found it?" Dad folds his arms. "Because I would love to hear this."

"I think I can explain." Luca only reaches out when my mouth falls open and covers my hand with his. His thumb slowly strokes my knuckles as he speaks. "It's the oldest story in the book. We fell in love. I love your daughter. She's the most important thing in the world to me."

"But how can you still be a detective and be with him?" Mom whispers. A server approaches but makes a sharp turn before reaching the table. I can only imagine how this must look, with Dad glowering and Mom clutching her throat with one hand.

Might as well get this over with all at once. "I want you to know I'm fine," I begin. They don't need to know it's a lie. "But I was injured. I'm fine now," I repeat when Mom whimpers.

"What happened?" Mom asks in a strained whisper.

"It happened while you were away. I was shot through the arm." The story Luca gave me rolls off my tongue. "I decided to resign. I'm not sure yet what I want to do going forward, but I'm comfortable for now." When all they do is gape at me, I shrug. "Well? You always thought I worked too much, right? You were always worried about me."

"Don't act like we're supposed to be happy about any of this." Dad removes his glasses and wipes them on his tie, shaking his head. "One day, you're a young detective, ready to take on the world. The next, you're showing up for dinner on the arm of a man—"

"A man who loves me," I remind him. Do I sound a little sharp? Maybe. Do I care? No, especially since his mouth snapped shut. "He loves me, Dad. It was just as complicated for him to bring me into his life. Things are still complicated."

"It wouldn't do Emilia any favors if word got around about us." Luca exchanges a look with me, and I couldn't be more grateful to see the calm assurance in his eyes. He's got this. I didn't know until now how much I needed him to back me up tonight. "So we're keeping things very, very quiet. In time, we can go public. Not now."

"Not so soon after my resignation," I insist when Mom's mouth opens. "People could get the wrong idea."

For the second time tonight, I'm about to tell a huge lie —or what feels like one. It's what they need to hear. It could even turn out to be true for some unimaginable reason. "I love him. I tried not to, for all the reasons going through your heads right now. It was impossible. I can't explain it any better than that." There's something painfully familiar about those three words that hit me square in the chest. Being here with Luca, his unwavering commitment, and me voicing that 'I love him,' feels strangely right, and I feel at peace for the first time since the hospital.

"Your daughter is safe with me," Luca assures them.

"I hope you don't expect us to accept this that easily." I hate the disappointed, weary frown my father wears. No matter how old I get, there will never come a time I don't want his approval. He's stood at the forefront of my ideals of honesty and fairness all my life, and he's disappointed in me.

"I'm not naïve, Dad." I offer a little smile to him, then to Mom. "But this is my choice."

Mom sips from her water glass then releases a shallow sigh. "Well, he grew on you. He might grow on us too." She straightens her spine and lifts her chin, and I don't think I've ever been prouder of her or loved her more than I do right now. Dad is about to say something when she pins him with a stare. "I'm starving. Let's get our menus so we can order, then we'll tell you more about the trip."

Luca squeezes my hand before signaling for our server. His eyes are twinkling when I meet his gaze, and I can't help but smile in relief. It's like we passed a test together, thanks to him, and I couldn't be more grateful.

If only everything could be settled so easily.

If only it weren't so hard not to drown in his dark eyes.

11

LUCA

"And they're going to be safe?" The anxiety behind Emilia's question is touching. There's genuine concern swimming in her eyes when they meet mine as she sits beside me in the car.

Covering her knee with one hand, I murmur, "Sure, they will. They'll be fine." They say patience is a virtue. Tell that to my hand where it is when what I want is to run my hand up her thigh until I'm between her legs, sinking my fingers inside her quivering pussy.

Either she's too busy worrying to care that I'm touching her, or she doesn't mind. "How can you be so sure?"

"Trust me. That's all I ask." She doesn't look convinced as she nods, settling back against the leather seat with a weary sigh.

"You did very well back there." I don't know why it feels necessary to encourage her. She's not a child, but she has been through a hell of a lot, and I couldn't help but love her if I tried. She infuriates me and challenges everything I thought I knew about myself, but none of that will keep me from loving her.

"You were the superstar," I scoff, but she doubles down, scooting closer to me. The effect is magic, warming my blood and making my pulse pick up speed. That's all it takes —simply having her close to me. "You saved the night. There aren't many people who can shut down an argument my dad is trying to make, yet you did it."

"I wanted to make sure they knew the score. All I want is to love you." It's getting easier to say things like that, though not much. I can still barely manage to get the words out without flinching, cringing at my awkwardness. It's pitiful and not something I'm practiced in.

She's worth bearing a little embarrassment. Sitting with her at dinner, holding her hand, it was all a reminder of why I was unable to get her out of my system no matter how I tried. Knowing she was wrong for me, I was helpless to do anything about it. It is too easy to love her.

She blushes and lowers her gaze before suddenly letting out a yawn so wide that I'm surprised it doesn't dislocate her jaw. She laughs at herself before shrugging. "I guess I didn't get much sleep last night. I was a little nervous."

"You'll sleep better knowing there's nothing to worry about." I, on the other hand, am sick to death of staying in the main house. It's comfortable but not nearly as comfortable as I'd be lying beside her. I know she's safe, yet all I can do is worry and want, rubbing my dick raw out of frustration.

"You look tired too," she observes. I didn't realize she was studying me until she notes her gentle observation.

"I'll be fine." Especially while she's this close, smelling as good as she does, looking like sex on two legs, even though she chose a modest dress for dinner. If anything, she's sexier this way, more tempting than ever. "Why don't you close your eyes?" It's clear she's fighting to keep them open.

"Maybe I will. It's like now that it's over, all I want to do is sleep." My heart skips a beat when her head touches my shoulder. It's the simplest gesture, yet it means everything. It isn't long before her breathing slows, and her body goes limp against me. It makes me consider telling the driver to take the long route. I don't want to give this up.

Stop being a fucking child. Rather than indulge my little fantasy, my thoughts turn to the business of keeping the Washingtons safe. I didn't bother telling Emilia about the detail I assigned them since she almost blew up when I suggested keeping them under surveillance.

I feel a hell of a lot better with eyes on them. That's more important now than ever since they've been out in public with me. It didn't seem like there were any threats in the restaurant, and we kept our plans quiet. I can't let her fears paralyze me. I know what I'm doing.

Is there any way to feel confident about what you're doing when you love someone?

Her head is still on my shoulder when we roll through the gates. I hate to wake her when we stop in front of the house since it means losing this moment and the trust that goes along with it. I can't help but take the opportunity to stroke her silky cheek, half-hidden by hair. My hand trembles when I remember everything we've come so close to losing. I can't allow it. I can't let her slip any further away.

"We're here." I give her a gentle nudge that makes her stir, blinking sleepily.

"Already?" She fights to rouse herself and needs a hand getting out of the car. "Wow, I really dropped off fast," she mumbles.

"I'm sorry I had to wake you up."

Fuck, is she tempting, leaning against me and yawning as I unlock the door. She's warm and trusting now, and I don't know whether my performance at the restaurant is the reason why or if it's simply that she's too tired to think. Not that it matters. I get to lead her inside and walk her to the bedroom, where she immediately kicks off her heels and lets her coat drop to the floor.

There's something wild in her eyes when they meet mine—something I've missed. "Do something for me?" she asks, turning around and brushing aside the loose, golden waves flowing down her back. "Unzip me?"

I don't know if she's trying to seduce me or what, but it's working. Not that she would have to try hard. As it is, I have to remind myself to breathe as I lower the zipper to her waist, revealing her creamy skin, all of it practically begging to be touched.

I would swear there's an electric charge in the air by the time she turns back to me, swaying a little, brushing against my chest. "Thank you."

"I do what I can." My voice is hoarse, and my chest is so tight it's a struggle to take a breath. The way she's looking at me, her warmth, her familiar body, it's all working together to make it impossible to hold myself back.

The thing is, I would swear she doesn't want me to. "Do something else for me?"

"Anything," I vow.

"Stay." With that, she lets the dress fall, the fabric pooling at her ankles to reveal her luscious tits encased in a strapless bra that matches the lacy thong she wears.

"And do what?" I have to ask. I can't help it. My hands settle on her hips, and she closes her eyes, sighing softly.

Then she winds her slim arms around my neck, one hand cupping the back of my head so she can pull me down into a soft kiss that doesn't stay soft for long. There's no hope of that, not when an inferno erupts when her juicy lips meet mine.

My tongue slides against hers, and she moans, opening her mouth wider so I can probe and explore while her fingers run through my hair. I can't help but touch any part of her I can reach—her silky skin and the goose bumps that erupt over her arms, shoulders, and back. By the time her ass rests in my palms, she's moaning helplessly, offering no resistance as I back her up against the bed, then sit her down.

I slowly sink to my knees, letting my hands play over her curves before I break our kiss and ease her backward. She goes stiff, and her breath catches, but I undo her a little at a time, kissing my way down her body until she arches her back, offering herself to me. I reach behind her to deftly release the bra clasps, then take hold of her tits and thank whatever or whoever is making this possible.

"Fuck, you're beautiful," I groan out before taking one of her nipples into my mouth, my cock throbbing with every guttural moan filling the room. Her head falls back, and her legs wrap around my waist, pulling me closer. Demanding.

She's going to get everything she wants.

Once I've worked her nipples into tight peaks, she falls back onto the bed, and I continue my tour of her writhing body. With my tongue, I trace a line down to her navel. "Luca…" She moans, lifting her hips when I tug at the waistband of her thong with my teeth.

The scent of her arousal is overwhelming and only gets stronger when I've dragged the scrap of lace over her legs. She spreads them for me without any prompting, treating me to the sight of her smooth lips and the juices already glistening on them. Her short, sharp breaths fill my ears along with the pounding of my heart as I run my flattened tongue up her slit.

"Oh my God!" She grabs my head, pulling it against her pussy and grinding her hips. I would normally take the lead, but there's something electric about letting her take what she wants. My aching cock drips in my pants, and I use one hand to free myself while she rides my face, grunting and moaning in abandon, coating my chin with her sweet juices.

"So good... just like that..." she breathes out, tightening her legs around my head. "Ah... there, yes. Fuck!"

Fuck, yes, I'll do that. I will do anything she wants, fisting my cock and flicking my tongue over her swollen bud. "Yes!" she sobs out, hips bucking, legs tightening until she's squeezing my head. Tighter, tighter, I ride it out until she goes still in the final moment before her orgasm takes hold.

"Yes... oh God, yes..." Spasms wrack her body in the wake of pleasure, and every quiver of her dripping hole sends a fresh wave for my tongue to savor. It's been too long, and I've needed her too much to hold back now.

Once her legs fall open and she's caught her breath, she sits up and wastes no time peeling away my suit jacket. I stand to let my pants drop, and she takes hold of my cock, guiding it to her open mouth before I know what's happening.

"Suck it," I grit out, closing my eyes and sinking into the blissful sensation of her tongue running up and down my shaft, her lips sealed tight around me. She hasn't lost any of her passion or her skill. "You're so fucking good to my cock, baby." My praise makes her head bob faster until my world spins, and my balls begin to pull up, already on the edge.

Which is what cues me to take her by the shoulders and

pull back. "Let me fuck you." I take her chin in my hand and tip her head back. She's fucking gorgeous—flushed, lips swollen, lust dancing in her baby blues.

Her body does the talking, slowly sliding back along the bed until she lies flat with her arms outstretched. Hovering over her, between her thighs, I could cry with relief. She's mine again.

The instant I push inside her, I'm fucking home. All tight and perfect, I could explode in her right now, she's sucking me in so deep. She arches against me and almost deafens me with a surprised shout. "I'm coming!" she gasps out, nails sinking into my shoulders, her cunt clenching around my cock.

There's no taking my time. Instinct and need demand I drive myself deep, hard, and mercilessly. The bed rocks in time with my pounding strokes and the high-pitched gasps coming from Emilia. "Yes... oh, fuck, yes... harder..." Her legs close around my ass, demanding all of me, and I don't deny her. I give her all of me in a roaring release that shakes me from the inside out.

"Oh, shit!" She flinches under me, gasping. "When was my last Depo shot? I can't remember."

Neither can I. I don't know much about that and think she might have gone to the doctor once we got together, but I don't know for sure. "We'll be fine," I pant, rolling away from her. It wouldn't be the worst thing in the world for her to get pregnant, anyway. In fact, I wouldn't mind if she did after tonight.

The idea leaves me smiling as I roll away from her, triumphant. Whole again. She fits her heaving body against mine, and I hold her close. My woman. "I'm never letting you go," I tell her once I've caught my breath.

"You're going to have to." Her breath fans across my chest when she chuckles. "I'm not sleeping on top of the covers all night."

"Fine. We take a short break to get under the covers, but that's it." As an afterthought, I add, "And I'll let go of you to make breakfast in the morning."

She chuckles again. "I hope you've gotten better since you made me those pancakes." Her head snaps up, shock registering on her face. "Oh my God. I remember."

My heart skips a beat soon after having slowed to a regular pace. "What do you remember?" I ask, cupping her cheek.

"We were in a cabin." Her brows draw together. "Why were we in a cabin? I can see it in my head. You made pancakes for me."

I thought this night couldn't get better. "See? It's coming back. It's all coming back."

Yet when my arms tighten around her, she only pushes herself up on her elbow to stare down at me. "What does it mean?" What a shame something that should make her happy only causes her more distress. "Why were we in that cabin?"

Why now? Why, when everything was perfect for the first time in weeks? "It's a long story," I hedge.

"Do I look like I have anywhere else to be?"

"All right. I think you're well enough to handle it." Her throat works, but she maintains her steely gaze while I slowly stroke her back and choose my words carefully. "We were hiding in a safe house in the Poconos because, as far as my family knew, you could have been a Vitali spy. You were spotted at my club. Vitali thought you were doing recon, and... you saw something you weren't supposed to see. Long story short, both sides thought you were a threat."

Her brows knit together while she processes this. I can't tell if my story has frightened her. "Not you, though?" she asks.

That, I don't have to think about. I was a little too busy becoming obsessed with her to consider her a threat, not to mention I knew she had no evidence against us. "Not me. I wasn't about to let anyone hurt you, so I took you up there, and we hid out. Unfortunately, we were tracked somehow by Vitali."

She looks at her right bicep, studying her scar. "Is that where this happened?"

"It is." Lifting my head, I press my lips to the scar before murmuring, "Do you remember anything about it?"

Her brow furrows before she shakes her head. "No, but it makes sense."

"That's where it happened. I could have lost you, and I've never stopped blaming myself. I had no choice but to bring you here because you needed help. I wasn't about to trust anyone else with your safety, and it seemed too risky to take you to a hospital."

"I see." Her confused expression tells another story.

"Craig fixed it so it looked like the Vitali men kidnapped you, and he was the one involved in the shoot-out instead of me. So there was no hint of you being involved with me. Nothing to ruin your reputation." It's important to me that she knows.

"That's enough for now." She shakes her head hard before returning it to my chest. "I don't need to know anymore right now. At least I know where the memory came from."

"I'm here," I remind her, my hand running up and down her back. Slowly, she relaxes again. "I'm always here whenever you have a question. No more half-truths. No more trying to protect you from the past. It's time to start moving forward."

She heaves a sigh, and I'm sure she's about to answer, but instead, she whispers, "Let's get covered up. I'm cold."

12

EMILIA

"This would look great on you too." Guilia tosses a dress over her shoulder, not bothering to see where it lands. "What shoe size are you?"

"Eight-and-a-half. Really, you don't need to do all of this," I tell her, but my words fall on deaf ears. Her generosity is overwhelming.

She declared it was time to purge some of her closet and decided everything was going to go to me. I don't have the heart to tell her our tastes are wildly different. I'm only a handful of years older than her, but I feel downright ancient when I hold up a tiny scrap of a dress and can't imagine myself wearing it.

Not outside the bedroom, anyway. I'm sure it would drive Luca crazy, though he might feel differently if I were to remind him where I got the dress from. Nobody wants to hear they've been salivating over an outfit their little sister used to wear.

She only scoffs. "Are you kidding? This is fun for me. I always wanted a sister." I look up from the dress to find her slowly turning toward me, cringing. "Sorry. I'm not trying to be all weird or anything."

"You aren't being weird. It's sweet. And for what it's worth, I've always wanted a sister, too," I confess.

Her brilliant smile makes me smile in return. She's such a sweet kid who only wants everybody to be happy. Knowing she's here, a short walk from Luca's, has helped me feel normal. Having a girl to talk to, somebody with no ulterior motives and no reason to be kind other than for the sake of kindness.

Glancing at my phone makes my stomach sink, "Is that the time? Shit." I have to take the pile of clothes from my lap and place them on the bed, groaning at myself. "Craig will be here any minute."

Her nose wrinkles. "I don't like that guy."

Interesting. I'd love to hear all I can about him before he gets here so I know what I'm dealing with. "I didn't know you knew him."

"I don't," she says with a shrug. "I've never really talked to him, but I've seen him around. He gives me a gross feeling."

"From what I've heard, he's not somebody I'd want to be friends with," I agree. "Luca told me a little bit about him." And his slimy double-dealing, but I'll leave that part out. Guilia wouldn't get it. She's never been a cop.

"Why are you even going to see him?" she asks as she flicks another dress my way.

Because I want to be sure everything Luca told me is the truth. Knowing it might offend her, I can't bring myself to say that out loud. As far as she knows, everything's going well. I feel stronger, and I haven't had a headache in days. No blurry vision, either.

But there's always that question in the back of my mind.

Was this real? Or is Luca only telling me what he wants me to believe? While I don't exactly have faith in Craig's honesty, there's no reason for him to lie about this. I have to believe he wouldn't steer me in the wrong direction.

"We have history. We were partners. Who knows, maybe he can help fill in the gaps." I manage.

Maybe I'm completely naïve. I'm not even sure anymore if my own rationalizations hold water. If I'm telling myself what I need to believe because every day I spend here, getting to know Guilia and sharing a bed with Luca, I'm a day closer to settling in and accepting this as my life. There's still that tiny part of me that won't let go of the way I always believed things ought to be.

After promising to come back later for the clothes, I hurry from Guilia's bedroom and jog down the stairs, meeting Luca at the bottom.

His smile is bright and genuine, and I can't help smiling back. "I was just going to come up and get you," he explains. "Figured you girls might've lost track of time."

The brushing of his fingers against mine makes my stomach flutter. "It's like there's an entire store up there," I whisper, and he laughs indulgently.

I shouldn't let myself bask in the warmth of his laughter or the joy of his touch. This has to be wrong, the way the past several nights must have been wrong. Nights spent practically tearing each other to pieces before we practically fall unconscious from exhaustion. But Luca has this way of making me feel like I'm his. I'm special, wanted, but more importantly, loved by him. No matter how right it feels, I can't allow myself to indulge.

Maybe my body can...

... not my heart.

"Don't ever let her tell you she isn't spoiled." There's a lot of affection and fondness in Luca's voice and his gaze as he looks up the stairs. "A call came in from the front gate. He just got here."

So much for feeling breathless and giddy, my stomach now sinking like a rock. I have no reason to be nervous. I don't know the man, but I've been looking forward to seeing him ever since Rocco decided it would be safe. All the excitement over the shootout two weeks ago has faded in the wake of fresh, compelling news stories.

I observe a dark blue sedan pulling up in the front court-yard through the window next to the front door. "That's him?" I ask, shrugging into my coat.

"The one and only," Luca confirms. I don't have to guess at his feelings for the man, not when he sounds like he would rather get a root canal than see him.

When a tall, sandy-haired man in a long coat steps out of the car and looks up at the house, a surprised laugh bursts out of me. "I know him. I remember him."

Luca takes my face in his hands, and it doesn't occur to me not to lean into his caress. "Little by little, you're coming back to me."

He's right. It might almost be worth putting up with Craig if it means regaining everything I've lost. The dread that's gripped me all day dissolves, and I step outside, almost trembling in anticipation. What else can he help me remember? Finally, I might be able to get the answers I desperately need.

"There she is!" Craig calls out, beaming from ear to ear as I descend the wide stone stairs. "You look great. I was worried that you would be in bad shape."

"Sorry to worry you." When I reach him, he surprises me by giving me a brief hug. "I'm really feeling much better." Funny, but his touch has the effect Luca's used to, making me stiffen in discomfort.

"Do you remember me?" he asks as he lets go, and we stand face-to-face, our breath mingling between us. His gaze is intense enough to make me look at his chest like he's trying to see through me.

"I recognized you when I saw you."

"That's great news!" Another hug follows this, and again, I go stiff. I doubt we had this kind of relationship before. We weren't even working together long enough for me to remember him from the days before my attack.

"Come on," I offer once he releases me. "I need to stretch my legs." Really, I want to get away from the house, even if we can't leave the grounds. I don't want anybody overhearing any of my questions. I glance over my shoulder and see Luca staring at us through the glass beside the door. Suspicious, possessive—does it really matter which is the case?

"How is your memory?" Craig asks as we start across the gravel courtyard.

I shove my hands deep into my pockets and duck my chin against the cold before admitting, "Patchy. Sometimes things pop up, always when I least expect them."

"Do you remember anything about the abduction?" When I flinch and hunch my shoulders, he makes a sympathetic noise. "Sorry. That was the wrong way to phrase it."

Something about his apology makes my hackles rise. "It's fine. I'm not a baby. I can handle it."

His sudden laughter confuses me worse than ever. "It's good to see some things haven't changed. You sound exactly like the Emilia who drove me crazy when we worked together."

"I do?"

He rolls his eyes before laughing again. "Please. You always knew best. It wasn't easy to keep your ass safe, always running headfirst into everything."

Okay, that sounds like me. "You don't have to worry about that anymore," I remind him. He doesn't need to make it sound like I was such a liability. I'm being touchy, but I have to wonder how well we could've gotten along. It doesn't sound like he liked me very much. Yet there he is, making a big deal out of coming to see me. Luca said he's been asking ever since I got out of the hospital.

"Things are a lot quieter without you, that's for sure," he admits, kicking a few stones out of the way when we reach the dead, frozen grass. "That doesn't mean I'm not sorry to see you go."

"Luca told me about the story you made up to cover for what happened... my injury," I clarify when he looks confused. "Don't tell me you didn't end up with a commendation or anything for that."

"I did," he admits, chuckling as he crams his hands into his pockets and lifts his broad shoulders. "I won't pretend there was nothing in it for me. It doesn't mean I'm glad."

"Help me remember the way things were." Does it sound like I'm pleading? Maybe I am a little. "It's still foggy. Like I'm trying to tune into a radio station, and I can almost hear the music, but there's too much static to be clear."

His indulgent chuckle makes my hackles rise again, though I fight to conceal my reaction while he explains, "We were working on building a case. You were determined to put an end to them once and for all." There's humor in his voice, almost like he's making fun of me a little.

"I couldn't have made things easy for you," I point out. There's something off about him. It's unsettling, especially since I can't pinpoint exactly what is wrong. I couldn't describe it if I tried. He's just... off, somehow. Twitchy. Always looking over his shoulder to where the guards are watching. What is he so nervous about? I'm sure this isn't the first time he's been here.

"It was a real pain in the ass," he tells me flat-out. "I couldn't convince you to give it up. And look where it landed you."

"Are you talking about where I currently live or my injury?"

"Both. Is that so wrong?"

This guy is a real piece of work. It takes concentration and a few deep breaths to contain my irritation. "Considering you're on the family payroll, I don't think you have the moral high ground here," I quietly point out as we stroll across the lawn.

"Well, you still sound like yourself, anyway." When I lift an eyebrow, he explains, "That's exactly the kind of thing you would've said to me before."

"I only lost part of my memory. I didn't lose myself." I kick aside a small branch that fell from one of the trees, but it does nothing to ease my frustration. How did I ever work with this man? The sarcasm has me grinding my teeth. It's a good thing we didn't work together for very long, or else I probably would have cracked every single one by now.

"You never answered my question." I feel him watching me but refuse to show it. "Do you remember the abduction?"

"Not a thing," I lie. What is it that won't let me tell him the truth that I vaguely remember the room I was in, the men who cut my hair and beat me, and the fight we had at the house before they took me? Some instinct holds me back, and I know better than to go against it.

"It's probably for the best," he decides with a sigh. "You

wouldn't want to remember something like that. You'd be better off blocking it out forever." Why the hell does he care so much?

I come to a stop, and he does the same. It's time to drop the bullshit. "I need to know something. I need you to tell me the truth."

He looks me up and down and, I guess, takes me seriously since he finally drops the snarky, sarcastic expression he was wearing. "What is it?" he asks, and if I didn't know better, I would think he sounds suspicious.

"Was I undercover here? I'm serious," I mutter when he snorts. "I mean it. How did I end up here?"

His head snaps back, and he folds his arms before looking me up and down. "You mean Luca didn't already tell you?" he asks with a smirk. "I thought honesty was the most important thing in a relationship."

Fuck this. "Let me know when you stop having fun..." I snap, "... so we can have an actual adult conversation."

His brows lift before he whistles softly. "Listen to you. I'm glad to see you so strong and sure of yourself."

"I'm glad you're glad." He's insufferable. Imagine acting all snarky and full of himself when he has been accepting money from the Santoros to keep them safe. I guess he needs to feel superior, or else he might realize what a slimy piece of shit he is.

"You want to know if this all started as an undercover investigation?" he asks, looking serious again.

"That's what I asked," I grit out.

I can't believe this guy. He keeps me waiting, holding my breath, like he's having fun knowing I'm hanging on his every word. Finally, though, he shakes his head. "No. As far as I know, that's not what this was about."

I don't know whether to be glad or devastated. This was

my choice. I chose to be with Luca, not because of work but because I wanted him.

"You have to let it go," he murmurs after a few silent moments.

I don't bother hiding my irritation when I look up at him. He is wearing a knowing smirk I would love to wipe off his face. "Let what go?"

"Everything you thought you knew about yourself. You've got to let go of it, or else you'll never be able to move forward." He places a hand on my shoulder and squeezes surprisingly hard. "We all make our choices, kid. And really, it's not up to anybody else to understand them."

"Is that your way of defending yourself?" I ponder, tipping my head to the side. "You tell yourself nobody needs to understand why you decided to go on the take?"

His hand falls away like I hoped it would. "Just like nobody needs to understand why you decided to switch teams and devote your life to somebody whose family you were chomping at the bit to destroy." He sounds tired all of a sudden and maybe a little sad. I guess I'd be sad if I were him too.

"Craig!" The shout is followed by a sharp whistle that makes us both turn. Dante is standing on the back terrace and waves an arm over his head once he has our attention. "Get over here, now!"

I never thought I'd be so happy to see Dante. If it wasn't for his timely interruption, I might have no choice but to at least kick Craig in the shins for being such an unfathomable prick. I guess he needs to feel like he's done the right thing, and we're the same somehow. We never will be. If I'm here for love, that's a hell of a lot better than betraying people who are supposed to be my brothers and sisters on the force for a little bit of money.

Maybe I'm the one trying to defend myself.

"I've got my orders." His lips are set in a firm, grim line when he looks my way again. "Take care of yourself, all right? I'll be back around to check on you."

I want to tell him he really doesn't have to go to the trouble, but he's already walking away. I can't say I'm sorry to see him go.

The little shiver that runs through me has nothing to do with the cold temperature. There's something off about him. I can't put my finger on it, and I could be imagining it. I don't think so, though. He was too intense. Hanging on my every word. Why? I don't get the feeling we were particularly close, even if we were partners. Maybe he was only trying to be polite but is too socially awkward to have it come off the right way. That's not a crime.

Luca meets me halfway to his house and wraps an arm around my shoulders as we fall in step together. For the first time since I set eyes on Craig, I feel relaxed. "How did it go?" he asks.

"Fine, I guess." I know I sound sullen, but I can't help it. What did I expect? For Craig to unlock everything I can't remember?

"You guess?" There's a growl under his words, and for once, I like the sound of it. "Do I have to kick his ass? Say the word."

I can't help but giggle. "No, you don't have to kick anybody's ass."

"Because trust me when I tell you, I wouldn't mind."

I can tell he's trying to cheer me up, and affection swells in my chest in response. If only I could shake the weird feeling I have. Is there something I'm missing? Maybe. Maybe my subconscious is trying to tell me something, only

I don't know what. All I can do is hope it's nothing critical, or else I could be in trouble.

"I don't like him," I decide.

"Like I told you before, you had mixed feelings toward him. He lied to you and undermined you." He snickers as we reach the front door. "Even if it was for my family's sake, I hate him for it."

Maybe that's it. Subconsciously, I know I can't trust Craig, and it's hard to like anybody I can't trust. That has nothing to do with my head injury.

We're barely inside before Luca takes me by the waist and hauls me in, growling. "What is it about watching you with another man that makes me want to fuck you senseless?"

As always, a blaze erupts in my core. It's like he knows the magic words to effortlessly turn me on. "Remind me to spend more time chatting with other men, then," I murmur, grinning when his eyes narrow dangerously.

For once, the idea of forgetfulness sounds pretty good and the sort of forgetfulness only Luca can provide.

13

LUCA

"I'm taking Vinny and Bruce with us up to the house. We'll be gone today and tomorrow. My idea was to return tomorrow night after dinner." It's unusual for me to drop spur-of-the-moment plans in my father's lap, but it only occurred to me last night while Emilia slept in my arms that going back to the Hamptons might be what it takes to bring back the rest of what's been lost. To call it a calculated risk would be putting it mildly, but it's either taking the risk of existing in public or waiting for Emilia's memory to return.

My father eyes me from behind his desk, his fingers tented under his chin. "So long as you know what you're doing," he reminds me in a quiet but heavy voice. "I would hate to see her lose ground when she remembers what happened the night she was taken."

He isn't advising me against anything I haven't already considered. "I know it could backfire," I admit. "But it might help bring everything else back. Besides, it would be nice to be in new surroundings for a while now that things are going well with us again."

He holds up a hand, chuckling softly, and while I didn't need to be reminded of why it was important to have this conversation one-on-one rather than involving anyone else in the family—meaning Dante—I'm comforted by his understanding. "Say no more. The things we do to keep our women happy."

I would tell him it's not like that, that she hasn't demanded or asked anything from me beyond honesty, but the clock is ticking. It would be a good idea to get the hell out of here sooner rather than later. Especially since Papa is the only person I've discussed this with, and I would rather not be around for Dante's inevitable temper tantrum when he learns I've ducked out for the day.

He wouldn't understand. He's never had a woman of his own for longer than a night or two. He wears it like a badge of honor, which baffles me. It was one thing when I didn't have time to bother with women, though I didn't brag about it. It wasn't a point of pride. For someone like my brother, whose entire identity is wrapped up in what he can do for the family, it's a welcome sacrifice. It makes him look dedicated. Obsessed, if you ask me, but then he knows better than to ask for my opinion on the way he chooses to live.

"How are you feeling?" I ask before leaving.

Emilia is waiting for me, both excited and a little apprehensive about our sudden trip, and I don't want to run into Dante. Yet I can't leave without making sure there's nothing I need to know.

He shrugs, scowling a little at the question. "Fine. What's with you hovering over me like this?" he grumbles. I can't say I love the irritation I hear, though it does mean he's feeling like himself again. I don't have time to respond before he checks his watch and continues, "I have a phone call in a few minutes. Is there anything else you want to talk about?"

I have officially been dismissed. "No, that's it. I wanted to let you know where we'd be." Before I'm out the door, I turn to look at him over my shoulder. "Would you do me a favor?"

He lifts his brows in silent interest. After taking a quick look out into the hall to ensure no one will overhear, I murmur, "Keep this between us."

His scowl is as familiar as the room itself. "Since when do we keep secrets like that?"

Since my reason for living was abducted and nearly murdered, and I still don't know who to blame. "Please. That's all I ask," I reply before setting out. I'm not in the mood to get into it since I know he'll scoff if I share my suspicions. He wouldn't believe anything I had to say about Dante, anyway. I'm not even sure my brother is the one to blame for someone informing Alessandro of our plans. I want to believe he wouldn't betray me that way, but there's never any telling when someone's self-image is based on their job. That's all there is for him.

It's impossible for me not to reflect on some of the choices I've made in the past as I step outside. We're due for an unusually warm spell coming up, and I feel it in the air. It's about time—I'm getting sick of the cold. It's the perfect weather for a trip to the Hamptons.

Emilia is waiting in the car, smiling brilliantly when I join her. "Everything okay?" she asks, and I love the chipper sound of her voice, like a kid who was promised a trip to the toy store.

"Everything's perfect, including you." She smirks and rolls her eyes, though I would expect nothing less. She is perfect and always has been, and she's the last person who'd ever believe it.

Once we get on the road, she leans against me, fitting her body to mine. I drape an arm around her shoulders, pulling her in close. She's back. She is mine again. As Vinny drives and she hums along to the oldies I asked him to play for her sake, I find myself envisioning the future. The possibilities that faded after she was hurt come roaring to new life.

However, my joy is tempered when we arrive at the house. I can't take my eyes off her as she drinks it all in, gasping at the size of the place and its nearness to the beach while the guys bring our bags in, then retreat to the guest house. There's no moment of recognition, no sudden flash of memory. I don't know how to feel about it. Whether I should want it or not.

I told myself not to look at the stairs, so naturally, that's where my gaze falls as soon as we walk through the front door. They've been scoured since that night when I came in to find a trickle of blood drying on the riser. I'll never forget the way the red stood out against the stark white paint or the heart-stopping shock of realizing what I was looking at. The implications. That terrible, sick feeling that flooded my body and left me unable to process anything in the wake of terror.

This isn't the time to stand around and dwell like a little bitch. My attention turns to Emilia, who is walking slowly through the living room, admiring everything the way she did when we were first here. There's a faraway look on her face. She moves slowly, taking her time as she runs a hand over the mantle, then turns toward the windows over-looking the beach without saying a word.

What a bizarre time for me to remember what's usually

said about sleepwalkers. How you're not supposed to wake them up. She's not sleepwalking, but she is deep in thought just the same. I don't want to interrupt, though everything in me wants to know what she's thinking and feeling. Remembering, if anything. What is she going through? She knows I'm here for her, doesn't she? I haven't left any room for doubt.

"This is all so beautiful," she eventually murmurs, and it's a relief when she turns my way wearing a smile. I can breathe. Tension I didn't know I was holding in my shoulders and neck eases. "Just beautiful. So peaceful."

Yes, and what a shame that peace was ruined. "I'm glad you like it. It sits here empty so much of the time."

"That's a shame." She looks up at the ceiling high above her head before turning in a slow circle, then shifts her focus toward the beach again. "Somebody should be admiring this all the time. Every day."

"You mean the way I admire you every day?" I ask.

She turns to me as I approach, smirking over her shoulder. Her blue eyes sparkle like the rippling water beyond the windows when she asks, "How do you do that?"

"Do what?" I ask as I unbutton my coat, draping it across the back of the sofa on my way across the room.

She follows suit, leaving her coat on a chair near the window. Her white sweater glows in the abundant sunshine pouring in, and between it and her golden locks, she could easily be an angel. "You turn the most casual observation into a chance to compliment me."

"It's not so hard to do when there's so much to compliment," I point out, brushing aside the hair closest to her neck so my lips can touch her soft skin. It might be sacrilege, touching this precious angel. I am not a holy man. I've done terrible things and will do so in the future. I don't deserve this.

Yet I can't resist, especially when she giggles and wriggles against me so temptingly. "You are a smooth talker," she whispers as I continue teasing us both. I can't help it.

"You don't seem to mind." With my arms around her waist, I pull her against me so she can feel the erection stirring in my pants.

"Why don't you ask the question I know is on *your* mind?" She's not giggling or squirming anymore when she pulls back to look me in the eye. Her gaze has an almost weary awareness as it travels over my face.

"What do you think that is?" I ask, trying to keep a straight face to disguise the uncertainty still bubbling in my gut. Is she going to suddenly freak out? Was this the right decision? I can't distract her with sex for the next thirty-six hours, no matter how much I'd like to.

This was going to come up eventually.

"Don't bullshit me," she whispers, both loving and defiant. "You want to know if I remember the attack."

How can she talk about it so casually? She's so matter-of-fact that I can only study her closely at first, wondering if she's putting on a brave face for my sake. Then again, what am I worrying about? This is Emilia, *my* Emilia, and while I can't go for very long without needing to touch her, that's not what lies at the heart of us. She is not only the hottest but also the most desirable woman I've ever set eyes on. She's brave, tough, and made for me.

That doesn't make me want to protect her any less. If anything, it heightens my protective instincts. I want to protect her from the memories. I want to spare her even a moment's pain.

Her penetrating stare won't let me shrug off the subject.

"Do you remember?" I venture, stroking her cheek with my thumb while my eyes move over her face, searching for any sign of emotion.

She slowly shakes her head, her brow furrowed like she's thinking hard. "I do have these little flashes of memory," she explains, looking over my shoulder, taking in our surroundings. "There's a pool past the kitchen, isn't there?"

"A pool we swam naked in," I confirm with a grin. "Before doing other things." It's amazing that my heart can beat, and I can breathe. I get the pleasure of watching a miracle unfold every time she brings up another scrap of the past.

"I remember being happy here." She's radiant when she smiles, standing on her tiptoes and brushing her lips against mine. How is it that every kiss is still as exciting as the first time? It seems like the thrill has to wear off eventually, right? But here I am, already lost in her, with everything else falling away so I can concentrate on the feel of her body and her soft sighs as I kiss her slowly, deliberately, like a man with nowhere to be and nothing better to do.

"Remember this?" I ask between kisses as I pull her down along with me until we're on our knees in front of the fireplace. It's cold now, dark, but the heat between our bodies is more than enough.

"I'm not sure." She wears a knowing grin when she pulls back long enough to lift her sweater over her head. "You'll have to remind me."

14

EMILIA

It seems strange, feeling sad after waking up to a brilliantly sunshiny morning, lying in what has to be the most comfortable bed imaginable.

We're going home tonight. The clock is ticking. I wish I could always be like this, just the two of us, without any family drama or danger hanging overhead. Things are so much simpler when we are alone together.

The sunshine streaming in through the French doors isn't enough to wake Luca, sprawled out on his back with his face turned away from the glass, one arm thrown over his head. This is not the first time I've woken up by his side, so it doesn't seem right that the sight of him takes my breath away and makes me feel all warm and needy, deep in my core. No matter how many times I see him like this, I can't get used to it. The finely chiseled abs, the thick shoulders, and the bulging biceps. I want to trace the letters inked across his chest just to test the firmness of the muscle underneath, but it's more important to let him sleep undisturbed.

I'm starting to understand how I fell for him in the first

place. He's a different person when he isn't acting all growly, possessive, and obnoxious. When he lets the mask drop and allows me to see his humanity, I like who I see—someone who's thoughtful and determined to give me everything I want. He's intelligent, too, and more than once, it's struck me as almost sad that all that intelligence is wasted on his family business. He could be something on his own if he wanted, but I don't think it would be possible for him to break away. Given the chance, I don't think he'd want to, either.

I can't look at his life through my eyes and expect him to see things the way I do when we were raised in two different worlds. Deep down, when I listen to the voice in my gut, ignoring the noise around us, I sense goodness in him. Sure, there are moments when the not-so-good and the down-right ugly outweighs it, but at his core, he's decent. He loves his family, adores his mother and sister, and practically worships his father. He would do anything to protect the people he loves.

So what if I don't agree with the methods?

I'm not blind, and I'm not stupid. I know exactly what I'm doing as I lie here cocooned in blankets so soft, it's unreal. The entire room is glowing the way Luca's skin does in the morning light, and I have no doubt that's coloring my thoughts, along with the persistent throbbing between my legs after spending most of yesterday going crazy on each other. Like we're making up for lost time, which I guess we are.

I'm rationalizing my feelings, letting myself fall for him again. Maybe it's inevitable, the way he likes to describe it. Like we're meant to be, a force of nature, something there's no denying. It would be like trying to defy gravity. Could it really be that simple?

He mutters something in his sleep, shifting a little, and the blanket draped over his midsection slides further down over his rippling muscles. His enticing happy trail leads my eyes downward, and it's all I can do not to lick my lips. This is not me. I don't lust like this.

Yet here I am, holding my breath as I lift the blanket away from Luca's hardening dick. It twitches a little as I watch. He groans softly, turning his head from one side to the other, with his eyes still closed and a soft snore emanating from his parted lips.

I can't help it. He is the living, breathing symbol of desire. He does something no one ever has done to me. It's like I've stopped thinking. All that matters is being close to him, touching his body, begging him to touch mine.

Slowly, I push myself up on my knees, then lean down to guide his swollen head into my mouth. There's something almost wicked about it, and by the time my tongue sweeps along the ridge, wetness pools in my pussy.

His throaty groan only adds to my growing arousal. "Oh, shit," he whispers, groggy. When I look up at him, I find him looking down at me, dazed but clearly enjoying the treatment. "Did I die and go to Heaven?" he mumbles before falling back against the pillows.

All I can do is chuckle, slowly fucking him with my mouth, taking my time. I want him to feel everything, every moment of it, every inch of my tongue running along every inch of his rigid cock. I could live on the sound of his pleasure, the way he whispers as I work him.

"Fuck, yeah, that's it," he whispers, his breathing going fast when I increase the pressure. "You're so good to me. You're so good to my cock. Suck it, baby." There's a helpless edge to his voice, and I love it. I want to hear him beg me for more. I want to render him helpless, at my mercy.

It isn't long before his hips start working, and his urgency makes me pull back with his disappointed groan ringing in my ears. The groan is cut off when I straddle him, dropping the blanket from around me so he can run his hands over my bare skin. I shiver when the head of his cock brushes my aching clit, and the sensation is electric enough to make me grind my hips, running his dick through my dripping slit until we're both breathing heavily.

"Fuck me," he growls out, fingers pressing against my hips before dragging over my thighs. "Let me feel that tight pussy wrapped around me."

All it takes is a slight adjustment for his head to line up with my entrance, and I release a guttural moan as I impale myself on his rigid dick. The angle is exquisite, and already, little shocks of pleasure rock me with every stroke. I rest my hands on his chest for leverage, then let myself go, focused on the delicious friction.

"Look at you." He takes hold of my boobs, pinching the nipples, squeezing my flesh until I whimper my approval. "So fucking sexy. Ride my cock, baby. Put on a show for me."

And I do, my hips rising and falling before grinding against his pelvis. I open my eyes to find him staring down between us, watching as he disappears inside me again and again.

He wants a show? I'll give him a show. "Holy shit," he growls out when I lean back and prop myself up on his knees. This angle is even better, my head falling back as another guttural cry tears its way out of me when his head rubs my G-spot.

"Fuck!" I shout, working faster, chasing the high that's just beyond my reach. "Fuck, yes! So good!"

"Are you going to be a good girl and come on my cock?" He punctuates the question with a thumb against my clit, rubbing it in short, rapid strokes that take my pleasure and make it explode. I can barely hear his commands over my high-pitched gasps. "Come for me. Be a good girl and come all over me."

"Luca! Oh God! I'm... I'm..." When it hits, I don't have it in me to speak. I can only cry out in complete abandon and fall against his chest, dazed and weak. Luca takes hold of my hips and works me up and down his shaft until he slams me down with one last groan and brings a satisfied smile to my lips.

His breathless laughter stirs me from my happy haze. "Holy shit," he groans out, and I lift my head from his chest, sighing at his tender kiss. "Where the hell did that come from?"

I lift a shoulder, smirking. "Maybe I've turned over a new leaf. It's all your fault for looking so good while you sleep."

His arms close around me, holding me tight against his chest. "Remind me to look that good every morning."

"I WISH we never had to leave." I squeeze Luca's hand a little tighter while we wander through the shopping village after a dinner so enormous that I'm not sure I'll ever eat again. But I am happy—full, a little buzzed from wine, and with a man I'm falling for a little bit more every day. A man who is so handsome, I almost can't stand to look at him sometimes. I don't know what to do with all that beauty.

"Same here," he agrees. He's smiling, happy, and light-hearted, making it easier for me to feel the same way. If only things could always be this way.

"That doesn't sound ungrateful or anything, does it?" I ask. "I don't want you to think I'm not grateful."

It doesn't seem to bother him that Bruce and Vinny are trailing half a block behind us. He comes to a stop, which brings me to a stop along with him, then cups my chin with his other hand. "Are you kidding? If we could stay here for the rest of our lives, I wouldn't complain. I love seeing you here. I love being able to leave everything behind us."

Not everything, it seems. Just as he's about to lean in for a kiss, he straightens. His eyes were so soft and loving a moment ago, but now they go narrow as he stares at something over my shoulder across the street.

"What is it?" I start to turn, but he stops me and shakes his head.

His eyes are nearly hidden by his lowered brow by the time he mutters, "Let's go." He looks back at the guards before nodding slightly toward whatever caught his attention. From the corner of my eye, I see Bruce crossing the street while Vinny remains watchful behind us as we continue our walk.

It's all wrecked now. Luca's entire demeanor has changed. He's gone from holding my hand to grasping it almost painfully tight. We were walking a minute ago. Now, he's almost dragging me along with him.

A chill runs down my spine before I whisper, "What's wrong? Did you see something bad?"

"Just keep walking." He doesn't look at me and barely opens his mouth when he speaks. We're coming to the edge of the village, after which we turn down the street leading to the beach, then it's a straight shot to the house.

We're supposed to leave tonight, so our bags are packed and ready to go.

Except instead of turning right at the end of the block, Luca continues leading me straight ahead. I'm too nervous to ask what the hell is going on. It's not like I'd get an honest answer, anyway. His long stride means I'm almost jogging to keep up. He doesn't seem to notice.

Across the street, I see Bruce closing in on a young man dressed in black pants and a puffy coat. He's wearing a knit hat pulled low on his forehead—no big surprise since it's pretty cold. From the looks of it, he's walking while doing something on his phone, and the glow from the screen is visible from a distance.

Suddenly, Bruce takes hold of the kid from behind and shoves him into a narrow passage between two darkened storefronts. Many of the little shops and boutiques in the village close early on weekdays. I guess because it's the off-season, there isn't much point in staying open until eight or nine o'clock when there's nobody coming in.

"What are we doing?" I ask when we suddenly change course, with Luca pulling me across the street. The few pedestrians also out and about don't pay any attention, though I wonder if they would if I screamed. Is this a scream-worthy situation? I'm not sure, but I'm starting to get an idea I won't like what's about to happen. It's the way Luca's energy shifted and the fact he has yet to answer my questions about what the hell is going on.

Vinny joins us by the time we reach the dark passage where Bruce has basically pinned the kid against a brick wall with an arm to either side of him. It's like he's in a human cage, trembling and wide-eyed. He can't be more than eighteen years old and has probably never been in a situation like this. "Wh-what's happening?" he asks, breathless.

Luca ignores the question. "Good work, Bruce." It's almost a relief when he releases my hand since he was squeezing hard enough for me to now flex my fingers and wince as blood starts flowing again.

"What is this about?" I whisper while he glares at the kid.

I might as well not be here. There's no reaction to my question. Instead, Luca nods to Bruce, who wastes no time slapping the kid's phone to the ground before shoving his hands into the kid's pockets and pulling out everything he finds.

"That's my stuff!" the kid protests weakly, like he's afraid to say anything but has to. He's terrified, and I can't say I blame him. This must all seem like it's coming out of the clear blue.

I'm afraid, too, except I have to say something. I can't stand here and watch this without trying to end it. "Why are you doing this?" I whisper, tugging Luca's coat, hoping to get his attention. He only offers a brief scowl, like I'm a pest, while Bruce goes through the kid's things.

"What, you didn't think I would notice you?" Luca gets in the kid's face, looming over him, and I hear the rapid, panicked breathing getting louder. "You were practically attached to us the whole time we were eating dinner, and then you get off your shift as we're leaving? What, I'm not supposed to notice that? Huh?"

The kid's mouth falls open before his head shakes almost violently back and forth in denial. "I don't know what you mean!" He might be trying to scream, but it comes out as a breathy gasp.

Now I realize Luca's right, that the kid worked at the restaurant where we had dinner. I noticed him walk past with a tray of used plates at one point, but for the most part, I was more interested in Luca than anybody else.

None of that means he's a plant by the Vitali family. "This isn't right," I murmur, grabbing Luca's arm this time.

"Take her back to the house," he growls out before practically shoving me into the breathing wall of muscle that is Vinny, almost like I'm an afterthought—something for him to push aside.

"What are you doing?" I ask again when I find my balance, but my questions fall on deaf ears. He doesn't hear me or doesn't want to.

"Now. Back to you." The kid yelps a little when Luca takes him by his coat and slams his back against the wall. "Who are you working for? Who told you to follow us?"

"I wasn't following you!" The kid is on the verge of tears, his voice shaking almost as hard as his body. "Please, I don't know what I did wrong! I work for my dad's restaurant!"

Luca leans in until their faces are almost touching. His snarl raises the hair on my neck, and I'm not the one he's snarling at. "Shut the fuck up," he grits out before pulling his right hand back. I recoil in horror at the sound of it striking the kid's cheek, and the sight of it turns my stomach. How can he be so effortlessly brutal, seeming not to hear the kid's pitiful pleas as he begins to slide down the wall?

"Oh, no. I'm not finished with you yet." A chuckling Luca hauls him to his feet. "You're gonna tell me what I want to know. Who the fuck are you? Who are you working for?"

"Don't!" I plead in the moment between Luca drawing his fist back and driving it into the kid's face. His weak, pained groan sickens me almost as much as the sound of fist hitting flesh.

"You can stop this anytime," Luca tells him over the sound of his suffering while Vinny holds me in place. "Just tell me what I need to know."

"Boss." Bruce holds out the kid's wallet. "He lives here. He's got the same last name as the restaurant and every-thing. It's his family's place."

"So what?" Luca fires back, wild and vicious. When he turns toward us, I forget to breathe. He's staring at us like we're strangers, wide-eyed, like an animal about to attack. "What, Vitali wouldn't hire somebody local? I told you to get her out of here!" he barks at Vinny, and I recoil when his gaze lands on me. He's a stranger again, someone I don't want to know, someone who would beat a stranger without stopping to wonder if he's making the right choice.

The kid slides to the ground, and his head lolls like a ragdoll when Luca shakes him, growling in his face. "Answer me!"

"We've got to go," Vinny insists, close to my ear. He holds my arm tight, but I barely feel it.

"Let go of me." I yank my arm away, and Vinny is smart enough not to take hold again. "Luca, you have to stop this," I plead, inching closer to where he now stands over the half-conscious boy. Luca did this without hesitating. He hurt this innocent kid.

He swings around when I draw near, hitting me with a death glare that makes me fall back a step. Like he pushed me without lifting a hand. "Don't you fucking tell me—" He realizes at the last second who he's talking to. I am not the enemy. Still, his teeth are bared when he mutters, "Don't tell me what to do."

THE INTENSITY of his glare pierces my vision once again, only this time he's wielding a hammer over a bloodied man slumped over in a chair. *Oh God.* That night we first crossed paths when I went to his nightclub. I recall trailing after him into his office, where...

Oh God, I feel nauseous.

"Somebody's gonna call the cops," Vinny predicts,

cutting through my memory. He leans out onto the sidewalk and looks back and forth. The man might as well hold up a blinking sign telling the whole town something bad is happening here. "We've got to go."

That seems to get through to Luca, who can't help but spit on the kid before he checks out the sidewalk the way Vinny did. "Let's go," he barks, taking my hand.

After what I've seen and remembered, I don't want to go anywhere with him. I can't exactly announce that out loud, though, and my head is spinning too fast for me to speak. I'm actually fleeing the scene of an assault on a completely innocent kid. All the happiness and hope I was basking in only minutes ago is gone, forgotten. The memory of this night has been tarnished forever.

Not only this night, either. Everything. He's ruined everything. Maybe I should be grateful to him for reminding me of who he is.

"I'm not making the same mistake I did before," he grunts out as we walk quickly toward the house, where the car waits for us. I'm glad we're packed and ready to leave. I'd hate to witness Luca paying off a cop to look the other way after what he did. It's bad enough I have to hold the hand that might have broken an innocent kid's nose. He did nothing wrong. His only mistake was crossing paths with a man whose temper is molten lava, always on the verge of exploding.

I'm almost glad he's too busy seething during the ride home to cuddle with me. I can't stand the thought of him touching me. While I could happily live without his energy stealing the air in the car, it gives me an excuse to sit as far from him as possible.

All I have to do now is figure out how to stay far away from him after tonight.

15

LUCA

As soon as I step into my father's office the morning after our return from the Hamptons, I know what I'm in for. He sounded pissed when he called my cell maybe five minutes after dawn, not that I was asleep. It was a long night spent staring at the ceiling and questioning myself, briefly punctuated by a few light naps.

It was obvious Emilia's attitude changed last night. We fell asleep wrapped in each other's arms two nights ago, with the sound of the ocean filling the air. Last night, she couldn't have gotten farther from me without falling off the bed. I spent hours on a king-size bed that felt a lot more like an island inhabited by myself alone.

In the end, I decided she'll get over it. She has to eventually see I'm interested in nothing more than keeping her safe. I won't leave her vulnerable again. If it means slapping some kid around, so be it. I'd much rather that than see her suffer again. No sacrifice is too great. Not for my love.

This mantra runs through my head on repeat as I consider getting coffee from the kitchen but head straight for his office instead. It wouldn't be a smart move to keep him waiting longer than I have, and I'd rather get this over with before my brother decides to come in and throw his unwanted opinions around.

Papa is sipping espresso from a small cup, standing by the window, and when he turns my way, his expression is neutral enough that I know I'm in for it. When he is beyond pissed, he goes quiet while other men might explode. The quieter he gets, the deeper his anger.

"Let's get down to it," I suggest, stopping in front of his desk and squaring my shoulders in preparation for what's bound to happen. "I figured one of the guys would report to you like the good little soldiers they are."

His slight scowl is the only sign he hears me as he lowers his cup to a matching saucer and sets both on the desk. "It's their job to report back to me. I know you believe they're your personal protection squad—"

"I don't," I interrupt, my hackles rising the way they always do when he gets this condescending tone with me. "As for last night, I did what I had to do."

His brows lift over widening eyes. "You smashed a kid's face in because it was what you had to do?" he asks in that deceptively controlled voice that tells me he's more pissed than ever. "You drew attention to us because it's what you had to do? Am I hearing you correctly?"

My molars grind as I take a slow breath. The last thing I need is to have Dante stroll in here to find us fighting. "I can't make you understand, can I?" I ask in a low voice, intended to cover up my irritation.

His sudden laughter doesn't make things better. "I understand perfectly," he tells me, spreading his arms wide before laughing again. "What, you think you're the only man who's ever worried about the people he loves? Do you think this is anything new? Like I haven't looked over my shoulder since the day I met your mother? Then, with each of you kids, my worries grew. There isn't a man in our position who doesn't know that dread. He lives with it like a tumor that can't be removed."

He lowers his brow and points a finger at me, his voice close to a growl. "He does not beat the shit out of a random kid who was working as a fucking busboy in a restaurant, and he sure as hell doesn't do it in public!"

It wasn't exactly in public. There were no witnesses, but I'm not going to bother arguing. "I did what I thought I had to do," I amend without moving or raising my voice, letting him see how serious I am and what this means to me.

At first, his only response is a soft sigh. "That's all any man can do," he agrees. "Which is why I want this war over."

His sudden shift is almost enough to make me scratch my head. "We would all like it to end," I agree. "As soon as we track down Alessandro—"

He waves a hand, cutting off my pointless reminder of where we are when it comes to the Vitali family. "I don't mean that. This eye for an eye shit? It doesn't settle anything. There's always gonna be somebody who wants to even up the score no matter what kind of truce is called. I wanted it over for good. Giorgio Vitali is still alive. He's still head of the family, no matter what that hotheaded kid of his thinks."

I can't believe what I'm hearing. "You're going to try to strike a truce?" I ask, almost afraid to put it into words. I want fucking blood, not a bunch of empty promises.

"If possible. Listen, Luca," he growls out when I open my mouth to argue. Now I see he's trembling with an intensity that leaks into every word. "One day, you'll understand. You'll be my age, and you'll be talking to your son. He'll look at you like he knows everything, he's seen it all and done it all, and you'll want to laugh at him because you'll know how wrong he is."

The flash of anger fades, replaced by what looks like sadness that hangs heavy in his voice as he slowly walks toward the leather sofa, gesturing for me to join him after he's taken a seat. "War is a young man's game," he quietly observes once I've sat with him.

He sighs deeply, staring toward a cluster of family photos dotting the bookcase across from us. It has the effect of releasing the air from the balloon. His face sags. Suddenly, I'm reminded of how worried I've been for him. It's almost like he's taken off a mask and is showing me his true self.

He offers a gentle, knowing smile when he meets my gaze again. "Don't tell me you want to spend the rest of your life worrying and looking for enemies everywhere you go."

"Of course, that's not what I want. I also don't want to back down now—"

"It's not backing down. We don't back down." His flash of irritation is like a sudden bolt of lightning flaring up out of nowhere. "It's doing the right thing for the future. For the people coming after us. This can't go on forever."

"I agree, but—"

He's not interested in letting me finish a damn word as he cuts me off. "I am still the head of this family," he reminds me. "If I say I want this over, that's how it's going to be."

It chaps my ass to ask this, except I have to. "Does Dante know?"

"Know about what?" he counters with a smirk. "That we're having a conversation, you and me? That's all this is," he adds, though I have to wonder if there's more to it when his smirk doesn't fade. "I've been doing a lot of thinking lately. I don't want you walking around worrying about your old man. One day, you'll understand what it's like."

I don't understand a damn thing since he isn't making any sense. "I thought you were calling me in here to give me hell," I admit, still wary.

"That was the idea, but I know it would be a waste of time. You're going to do whatever the hell you want when it comes to her." I can't tell if he's resentful or if he admires me for it.

"Tell me the truth," I urge. "Would you do any different if you were in my shoes, trying to protect Mama?"

The hardening of his expression is the same as a wall lowering between us. "I would've done a lot of things differently, but then you know that already." Dante's entrance marks the end of our conversation, leaving me to spend our usual morning meetings wondering what the hell that was supposed to mean.

Not that I need to wonder. I remember too well Papa's determination to get Emilia out of the way once and for all. I wish he'd keep that shit to himself, is all. I thought he'd changed his mind about us. I thought he saw my side of things.

It's still weighing on my mind when I take a break, heading down to my house to ask Emilia if she'll have lunch with us today. If not, I'm sure Guilia would be happy to come down and hang out with her. She shouldn't spend so much time alone. She needs to feel like she's a part of the family. One of us.

Immediately on stepping over the threshold, it's clear something is off. The photos and books that came from Emilia's apartment are absent from the living room. She's moving around in the bedroom, opening and closing drawers one after another.

I know what's happening, but that doesn't mean I want to accept it as I slowly walk across the room, closing in on the bedroom and the woman currently packing like her life depends on it. The door is open far enough for me to slip through without making a sound. She's working with her back to me, cramming items into a suitcase seemingly at random.

A shockwave rolls through me, strong enough to rock me back on my heels. So this is how it feels to live through a bomb blast. For one fleeting second, I wonder if I want to live through it because I know what I'm witnessing. Rolling my shoulders back and stiffening my spine, I ask, "What the hell are you doing?"

She jumps and spins in place, wearing a stricken expression like she's afraid she's made her last mistake. Her frozen shock lasts for a second before she gets a hold of herself again. "You're not usually back this early," she observes, her voice breathy, a handful of bras clutched against her chest.

Of all the things she could've said, that might be the worst. "What are you doing, Emilia?" I grit out again because the reality is if she leaves me again, I'm already dead.

She casts a look over the bed, where her bags are lying open, then looks down at the boxes stacked near her feet. "I'm leaving." When I can only stare at her, she adds, "This is what I need to do."

What she needs to do. I let out an exasperated huff. She needs to shatter my life? She needs to pack her bags while I'm out of the house like she's sneaking off in fear? "No, it's not," I insist. "You need to stay here with me. Where do you think you're going?" I can't believe this is happening.

"To my apartment, where I belong. I know..." she sighs

when I protest, "... I know you don't want me to go. I know you think I'm safer here."

"You are!" Her head snaps back at the volume of my voice, but I'll be damned if I tiptoe around to spare her feelings. I may have fucked up, but this... no, she can't leave me. "You're safer here, where I can watch you. What is it going to take to get that through your skull?"

I could've gone the rest of my life without hearing her derisive laughter. "According to whom? You?" She shoves the bras into the closest bag, then grabs a handful of socks from one of the drawers and adds them without looking, like she's fleeing in panic.

From me.

I'm the one who loves her, and she's fleeing from me.

"Yes, according to me," I snarl out, marching around the bed, taking the bag by its handle and pulling it to me. "You're not going anywhere," I insist, my tone strained with affection, though I can't shake the feeling of her slipping away.

"Listen to yourself." She shakes her head before taking hold of the bag and yanking it back. "You sound like the textbook example of an abuser when you talk that way. I'm not your prisoner." *So this is the game we're playing,* where she pulls a superior act like she's better than me.

The last drawer is empty. I slam it, taking her by the arms and turning her to look at me. I hate what I see etched across her face. The distrust. The dread.

"Let go of me," she murmurs, and it's somehow worse than anything she could scream. Flat, toneless, like she's talking to a stranger. The last thing I want is to cause her pain.

Somewhere during the night, she pulled away from me. She shut down.

And my world is shaken.

"How can you do this when we were so happy yesterday?" I ask, searching for something hidden in her eyes. It has to be there. I refuse to believe otherwise.

That's what makes her chin quiver and reveals what's going on inside her. She can't turn her feelings on and off. "But then last night happened," she whispers. Her jaw tightens, and her eyes go hard rather than welling up the way I expected. "You reminded me of who you are."

My fingers press into her flesh until she winces, but it's not enough to make me lay off. If I loosen my grip, I'll lose her. "I did that for you." I'm practically pleading with her now.

"Oh, please. Don't do me any favors." With a grunt of determination, she pulls herself free and turns her back to me. "This is what I need to do. If you love me, you'll let me do it."

I step up behind her, barely able to breathe. This cannot happen. But it is. "I could tie you to the bed right now and make sure you never leave," I murmur, tracing her waist with both hands, running them up and down before pulling her ass against my crotch. "You know I could," I add, knowing our attraction is the final thing left in my arsenal to keep her with me.

"And I know you won't." For once, she doesn't succumb to me. My heart goes cold and still as she zips up the duffel bag, then a small, wheeled suitcase.

This can't be happening. "Don't leave me, Emilia," I growl out. I hear the desperation in my voice, but what the hell? She knows what she's doing. What's the point of keeping my pride when the only person I give a damn about is ready to walk out of my life?

"I have to go. I knew you wouldn't understand. That's

why I wanted to leave before you came back. I can't stay here," she insists, and now her voice is shaking. She's losing strength. She doesn't want this, I know it. I feel it in the depths of my cold, heartless soul.

A flash of hope brings inspiration with it. "Then stay up at the house," I suggest, still speaking to the back of her head. "There's an empty room across from Guilia's or any of the other guestrooms. It doesn't matter which."

"You don't get it." Her head hangs low before she sighs, but her body is rigid. She's not about to give in to me. "I don't want to be with you."

The words take my breath away, but the way she delivers them slams into me like a wrecking ball. "You're lying," I snarl out as I spin her in place and lock an arm around her back, crushing her against me. "That's a fucking lie. At least have the balls to tell me the truth!"

"That is the truth," she states, her blue eyes piercing mine. Is that pity I hear? Somehow, it only makes things worse. "After what I saw, I don't want to be with you. I know what you thought you were doing, and I know you're going to use that excuse for the rest of your life. You hurt somebody? Killed them? Well, you were only doing what you thought you had to do to protect somebody you love."

"That's who I am."

Her brows draw together before she whispers, "Exactly."

"Don't pretend you don't want me." This is pathetic, beneath me, but I would do anything so long as she stays. I would lie on this floor and let her walk on me or use me as a punching bag, I don't care. I am not losing her again, especially not over something like this.

There's no denying that the light has left her eyes. All of the warmth, affection, and playfulness I saw in her days ago is gone. I extinguished that light because I thought she might be in danger.

"I won't act without thinking again," I vow, as close to blind panic as I've been since the night she was abducted. With my heart pounding and my stomach twisting, adrenaline is racing through my system and demanding I fight.

"You say that now because you would say anything to make me stay. It's not going to work. I am sorry," she insists, and her voice trembles again. "But I can't forget what I saw. I tried. I told myself to. I can't do it."

This isn't possible. I can't let it happen. I refuse. "Even though I did it because I thought I was protecting you?" I ask in disbelief.

"Even then." There's sadness in her voice, but she's firm. "I need you to let me go so I can finish. This is going to happen whether you want it to or not. I could make a phone call and have the police here in a heartbeat, along with my parents, my father's lawyer friends, and the local news. I don't want to do that." She holds my stare when she adds, "Don't make me do it, Luca."

"I love you, Emilia." It's the only truth I have to cling to as she backs away from me, pulling her bags from the bed while I feel like I've been through a hurricane. In a way, I have. My life has been flattened in the process, ripped to shreds. And I have no reason to rebuild.

"I know you do." Now a tear rolls down her cheek, which she quickly, almost angrily wipes away. "And that doesn't make this easier for me."

Her choice of words sets off a firestorm in my head. "What a fucking shame this can't be easy for you," I snap before picking up one of her boxes. "Let me help you. I'm sure you're in a hurry."

The pity in her eyes does something dangerous to me. I

can't be around her while my heart shatters to oblivion. "Take your bags outside," I growl out. "Put on your coat, get your purse. You're not stepping back into this house once you're out the door. I'll bring out the rest and have Vinny load up the car."

She hesitates for a split second before lowering her head and continuing through the house, stopping by the door for her coat. I step past her, dropping the box on the porch before whistling for Vinny. "Get the car!" I call out. "You're going to Brooklyn!"

Emilia groans softly from inside. "Luca, please..." I ignore her bullshit whispers, returning to the bedroom for the other boxes, laser-focused on getting through this. Living from one breath or heartbeat to the next is the most I can manage.

Stop her. The command rings out in my head like a gong, reverberating through me, but I know it's no use. I've already debased myself enough for her, and why? For what? For her to pity me?

Still, something holds me in place instead of letting me go straight to the porch with the other two boxes. I wait, watching as she looks around one final time before going out with her bags and closing the door behind her.

The click of the knob is all it takes to get me moving. I open the bottom drawer of my dresser, where the letters I've written her have sat unread all these weeks. She might not want to see me, but I need her to know we were always real and that I've loved her as much and as hard as I could.

After shoving them into a shoebox, I close the cardboard flaps and pick both boxes up. Outside, I find her talking with Vinny as he loads up the trunk. "Get her home as soon as possible, then stick around outside until I call you," I mutter, handing him the boxes without looking her way. I don't dare. I might do something terrible if I look at her.

Or something terribly humiliating, like begging her not to take away my reason for living. Instead, I watch from the front window as the car rolls away.

She walked out of my life without bothering to give me another chance. And with it, any love my black heart might have felt.

16

EMILIA

"Really, I'm fine." I hook a finger around one of the curtains over the front window and pull it aside a few inches, far enough that I can see the black car down at the curb. That car won't leave until the next vehicle shows up to take its place. At least, that's the way it's been the past few days since I came back to my apartment. I might have walked out, but not far enough for Luca to truly let me go. He insists on keeping guards outside around the clock, no matter how I feel about it.

Secretly, I don't mind. All it takes is a look at myself in the mirror, without my wig since I'm alone with no one to impress, to recall why a security detail might not be a bad thing.

"I wish I had a chance to say goodbye." Guilia's voice trembles, and the sound makes me wince. I didn't mean to hurt her by leaving suddenly. "You'll come back, won't you? This isn't for good."

I want to give her a little comfort, but I can't lie. She isn't a child. I don't have to tiptoe around her feelings. "I'm not sure. It's complicated."

She groans. "Want me to mess with him for you?"

It feels good to laugh, something I've done very little of lately. Not since our dinner in the Hamptons before everything went to hell. It hurts to remember that, so instead, I ask, "What would that involve?"

"Leave it to me," she says with determination in her voice. "I'll bug him until he realizes what an ass he is for letting you go."

If only it were so easy, but that's not something I want to get into, either. "Maybe take it easy on him," I decide. "He is going through a lot right now. And I'm fine," I insist before she can ask. "I really am. I need this time to myself."

"So long as it's not forever," she adds before we get off the phone. "I just got used to having another girl around here."

I can't say I feel much better once I'm off the phone, though how could I be at a time like this? I've barely unpacked, unable to muster the energy or care to get off the couch and pull my life together, even in the simplest ways.

This was my choice. That doesn't make living with it any easier.

Why did he have to do it? I've spent this time alone, trying and failing to wipe that question out of my mind. It's pointless, useless. There are no answers, none that matter, anyway. He did it for me, so he says. I think that's bullshit. I think he is way too comfortable using violence to get his way, and it doesn't matter who gets hurt. He has a way of rationalizing everything, and that is not the kind of person I want to be with.

Even if I do want to be with him, I want him with all my heart. When he's the version of himself he showed me in the Hamptons, I want nothing more than for us to be together.

When I'm with him, I feel whole. It's bizarre and inexplicable, but it's a fundamental truth.

The faint growling of my stomach reminds me I haven't eaten yet today. I know better than to order delivery. I doubt a delivery driver could get up here without being patted down by whoever is on duty outside. The groceries I picked up the day I returned won't last forever. I'll have to go out again, which means being followed around by yet another guard. I might as well wear a sign around my neck, inviting stares and whispers. These guys are not exactly the type who blend in. I guess that would go against the point.

After boiling a pack of noodles, I carry the steaming bowl into the bedroom. It's about time I finished putting things away. I can't move forward if I'm stuck in the past, with bags all over the bedroom and mostly empty drawers and shelves.

It doesn't take long for me to figure out that it isn't only being heartsick that's kept me from getting any further with this than I already have. It's the finality of the act. If I finish unpacking and set my apartment up the way it used to be, that means it's really over. I don't live with Luca anymore.

We aren't together anymore.

Only weeks ago, this was the outcome I wanted. To be here, on my own, living more or less the way I want to live. Granted, I could do without armed men watching me, but even that is something I could learn to live with.

Suddenly, a sweater isn't just a sweater. Placing it on the shelf in the closet is another step further away from Luca. This is the right choice. I have to believe it is. At the end of the day, I'm a possession he wants to protect. I'm important to him, yet so is his car.

A handful of shoeboxes are stacked in a cardboard box that is otherwise full of books and photos. I notice now that the lid to the top box doesn't quite fit, sitting crooked. I lift the lid and look inside to find a pair of shoes and a stack of folded paper—letters, by the looks of them.

I sit on the bed and open the first one to find a hand-written message on paper with the hospital's logo printed along the top.

Dear Emilia,

You're finally awake. They keep telling me you're going to get better. Once you recover a little, you'll get your memory back. I have to believe that's true, or else I don't know why I should bother living anymore. It sounds pretty sad, and before you, I would never have dreamed of thinking that way. Now that I have you, though, I know you're my purpose. The night we met, even when I found out you were a detective and were lying to me, I couldn't do anything but want you in my life.

Oh, my God. I remember that. Whether the memory has laid dormant inside me all this time or his letter dug it out of my brain, I don't know. I remember going to the club. I remember waking up in his office, scared out of my wits but also incredibly drawn to him.

My hands are trembling as I fold the page, setting it aside to pull out the next letter. It, too, is handwritten on hospital letterhead. I guess they must have had some in that waiting area where he spent so much time.

Dear Emilia,

You're getting a little better every day. I'm so proud of you.

Before now, I knew how brave and strong you are, and now you're proving it to everyone who takes care of you.

All I want is to take care of you too. I keep imagining how life will be when you're out of here, and we can go back to normal. There are so many places I want to take you, so much I want you to see. I want to experience the world through your eyes. You help me see everything in a new light. You give me a reason to keep moving forward.

Dear Emilia,

It's been four days since the doctors told me you lost your memory. It was like living in a nightmare when you didn't know who I was. You still don't know, but I'm not giving up.

That's another thing you taught me without meaning to. I know what it means to love someone so much that you would do anything so long as it meant it's what's best for them. I want to beg you to remember me. I want to remind you of everything we've been through and everything that's waiting for us, but it will only push you further away. As it is, you're miles from me now.

I'd give anything to hold you. To kiss you. I wake up at night with your name on my lips, ready to call out and beg you to return to me. All I can do is give you the space and time you need to heal.

I need you to know nothing is ever going to change my love for you. It will never go away or weaken. I'm going to love you to my last breath and probably beyond then. Nothing will ever change that.

THERE ARE SO many more written on lined notebook paper and scrap paper that may have come from his father's office or his mother's sitting room. Dozens of letters pouring his heart out to me. He wrote down everything he couldn't say out loud. He knew I wouldn't react well but couldn't keep it bottled up.

Even as I was leaving, he didn't tell me about them. All he could do was make sure I saw them.

According to the letter, he wrote the last one the morning we went to the Hamptons.

Dear Emilia,

I'm taking you back to the Hamptons. I decided last night that's what I need to do. You might remember being abducted, and it might be too much for you, but you're going to remember eventually. I would rather be with you when you do than have you remember it while you're alone somewhere, without me.

I had a dream last night that we lived together in the Hamptons house. All I wanted to do when I woke up was go back to sleep, but having you in my arms was better than any dream.

I hope you remember. I hope this is what it takes to bring you back to me. Having your body isn't the same as having your heart. It's your heart I'm still longing for. I'll never rest until I get you back. I love you so completely, I can't remember who I am without you.

I'm BARELY BREATHING as I lower the paper to my lap. It's a good thing his message was short since tears now blur my eyes and blind me to the room. What do I do now? I already believed he loved me in his way, even if love and possession tend to mean the same thing to him.

But reading the words he wrote straight from his heart is another story. Touching the paper where his pen indented the page, he poured himself out to me in these letters. He could've burned them after I left, but instead, he hid them where he knew I would find them.

He still believes in us.

My tears start dripping onto the page, so I put it with the others before wiping my cheeks with trembling hands. What am I supposed to do now? How do I turn my back when I know how he feels?

My heart jumps at a sharp knock against the front door. The guards don't usually disturb me when they're changing shifts. I don't need an announcement.

All at once, I jump to my feet, sure it's Luca. That he couldn't stay away another minute, like somehow, he knew I discovered his letters and would want nothing more than to hold him as soon as I read them.

Still, I hesitate before flinging the door open. "Who is it?" I call out before biting my lip.

"It's Craig."

Of all people. My heart sinks as quickly as it soared before I open the door to find my ex-partner standing in front of me. Right away, I sense something is wrong thanks to his scowl and what looks like a sheen of sweat on his forehead. "Are you okay?" I ask, opening the door wider for him to come in.

"I wish I could tell you I was," he says with a sigh. "But I'm afraid we have a very big problem."

17

LUCA

The knuckles of my right hand are bruised and a little swollen in the aftermath of a long and brutal questioning last night. It's been a long time since I've let my fists do the talking for me. Violence is never a problem, but over the years, I've become comfortable using weapons and tools rather than my right and left hand. That comfort is coming back to kick me in the ass as I walk to the kitchen to grab some ice and wince as I flex my hand.

Cesco's presence at the kitchen table surprises me. He's digging into a serving bowl full of cereal and barely looks up from it when I enter the room. "Hungry?" I ask on my way through.

"I figured if we're going out again tonight, I better make sure I eat plenty to keep my strength up," he retorts. I turn away from the freezer, ice in hand, to find him slurping milk straight from the bowl.

"You don't have to go out with me," I remind him as I wrap the ice in a towel and hold it to my knuckles. "I don't need anybody holding my hand."

"Who said anything about holding your hand?" he asks while carrying his empty bowl to the sink.

"You better not think about leaving that shit in there for Mama to find," I warn when it looks like he's about to walk away. "I'd gladly go out there and hunt down those Vitali pricks, but I wouldn't go up against my mother."

"You're right. I don't know what I was thinking." He's good-natured about picking up a sponge. "As I was about to say, you know I'd never say anything against going out and cracking a few skulls, especially if those skulls belong to anybody stupid enough to associate with those Vitali assholes." He spits into the sink for emphasis.

It does feel good to inflict a little pain, that's for sure. If only it got me anywhere. "I've been thinking about what that guy was saying last night when he was still conscious and talking," I add. There is something almost alarmingly satisfying in remembering how I broke him down. He managed to hold out through an entire hour of me pounding on him before he cracked and gave up what little information he had.

"You were able to make out anything he said?" Cesco asks, drying the bowl and putting it away. It's funny watching him do something so domestic when he held that pathetic, weeping prick on his feet for me to continue my interrogation last night. He did it while wearing a grim smile too.

It has bothered me throughout the day, the almost incoherent rambling once I punched and eventually kicked that asshole until he realized he had no way of surviving the night. "Something about paying somebody? What did that have to do with anything? Was he trying to say they have one of our guys?"

"It could be." My cousin shrugs but doesn't look away

when I give him a sharp look. If there's one thing I can count on, it's him looking me straight in the eye when he knows he is going to tell me something I don't want to hear. "It would make the most sense. We've gotten nowhere after all these weeks, questions, and beatings. Alessandro locks that shit down, man. He makes sure not to let information leak."

"Are you saying we do?" I ask as bile begins to rise in my throat. *Is he right?*

His head swings back and forth. "You're not listening to me. Vitali doesn't share plans with anybody who doesn't absolutely need to know about them. Up until now, we have gotten no information that led anywhere... and believe me, I was just as persuasive as you all these nights I've been out, looking under every rock and whore in New York." He gives my fist a pointed look. "How's the ice treating you?"

My cousin rarely inserts his opinion, and even more rarely does he speak this much at one time. That doesn't mean I feel like hearing it. "Get to the point."

"My point is, I have to believe the information we do get is the real thing. Like the info we got last night. I know we don't leak around here," he adds. "Which tells me if somebody did hand over info, they were paid to do it. Do I need to pull out a whiteboard and draw it for you?"

I've already considered this. It was one of several scenarios I weighed today since what else is there to do but absolutely anything that will take my mind off the crushing, numbing emptiness now that Emilia is gone. I can't bear to be down at the house now that she's no longer in it, waiting for me. It never felt empty before, but now it feels so cold and comfortless despite having every possible comfort at my fingertips. None of it matters. I would rather hang around here and go hunting for Vitali soldiers until I'm too tired to see straight than spend time there.

"Where are you going?" Cesco asks when I walk away without warning. Rather than answer, I let him follow me to Papa's office. The door is open, and the light burns inside, spilling out into the hall.

Dante sits on the corner of the desk, a glass of scotch in hand. His mouth snaps shut like my appearance leaves him unwilling to speak. It's no secret Emilia is gone, nor that my brother believed she should be here in the first place. I wonder how long he's spent gloating to our father over this turn of events.

Papa sits in his chair, his own scotch in hand. "Don't go ratting me out to your mother," he warns me. "I told her I would give this up."

"Sure, whatever," I mutter. I can't pretend to care as I nod to both of them. "Sorry to interrupt whatever this is, but there's something I think we need to discuss."

"What else is new?" Dante asks before staring pointedly at my iced fist. "Shouldn't you be out somewhere in the city by now? Maybe there's a cab driver you can beat up. Or a dishwasher."

My hackles rise at the mention of it. "No wonder we can't find Vitali, with everybody hanging around and gossiping like a bunch of schoolgirls. At least I'm out there getting my hands dirty instead of sitting here in an office and pretending I'm hot shit."

"I do not hear this, do I?" Papa shakes his head before scowling at both of us.

Dante barely glances at him. He's far too busy smirking at me, setting his glass aside before standing with his chest puffed out like he's hot shit. The sight disgusts me. "Don't pretend anything you've been doing has anything to do with this family. It's all about her, and everybody knows it." He sneers.

I take one menacing step toward my brother before Cesco places himself between us, facing Dante. "Luca and I were just talking about somebody we questioned last night. It wasn't easy to make out a lot of what he was saying by the time he started talking. A mouth full of broken teeth will do that to you, I guess." He snickers, obviously trying and failing to break the tension. "But we both think we heard him talking about somebody Vitali is paying. That's the guy we need to talk to, he said. He never used a name."

"Where is he right now?" Papa asks.

"He's in no condition to talk again. Don't worry about it," Cesco quickly replies. I doubt there's much of a question as to how our unfortunate informant ended up last night. "The point is, if Vitali is paying somebody to hand over information, this goes way further than Emilia."

Dante's brows draw together. I'll be damned if he doesn't look like a mirror image of Papa, who wears the same expression. "No. That's impossible," Dante murmurs, shaking his head. "We've never had a problem with that before, have we?"

He turns to Papa, who shakes his head. "Never. That's one thing we always made sure of back before my grandfather's time. Pay them well, take care of them, and they have no reason to turn their back on you."

But Frankie did, didn't he? My best friend, more of a brother than Dante ever was, betrayed the family who took him in and treated him as their own. Papa either forgets or doesn't want to think about it. Either way, the past remains the same. "Everybody has a pain point," I muse. "All it takes is finding it and applying pressure."

"Well, we know what yours is," Dante gloats.

"Don't pretend you don't have any," I snap back, trying

and failing to push past Cesco. "Stop acting like you're not human."

"I'm tired of this." Papa slams his glass onto the desk. "I hear what you're saying, Luca. And you're right. All it takes is knowing enough about a person to know how you can get to them."

"As much as you don't want to talk about this..." I growl at my brother, "... we need to. Somebody tipped Vitali off to that Hamptons trip. It sure as hell wasn't me, and there weren't very many people who knew about it. I can think of a few beyond the people in this room now. I sure as hell hope Mama and Guilia would keep it to themselves. Nico too."

"Did you speak to anyone else, Dante?" Papa asks in a quiet, almost gentle voice like he has to coddle the precious baby.

"Yes, underboss. Did you?" I echo. The ice bucket is open on the bar, and I drop what's left of my makeshift ice pack inside before flexing my hand. "I would like to hear about any conversations you might've had."

"Am I supposed to be threatened?" Dante asks. His chest puffs out farther, to the point where I worry about the buttons on his shirt popping off and flying around the room. The obnoxious shit.

The sight of his pompous bullshit makes my blood boil and burns away any last scrap of self-control for Papa's sake. "Who did you talk to, Dante?" I demand, charging at him and taking him by his collar to haul him in close. He bares his teeth, eyes hard and gleaming, and his lips sealed.

Papa stands, slamming his hands on the desk. "If the two of you don't stop this shit right the fuck now—" His warning is interrupted by the loud ringing from my phone. I made sure to turn the volume up in case an important call comes through, and now the sound jangles loudly enough for all of us to cringe.

It's enough to make me release Dante, anyway. I pull the phone from my pocket. It's Bruce calling, and the fact that he's scheduled to guard Emilia's apartment tonight makes my heart clench before I answer. "What happened? What's wrong?" I bark out.

Bruce sputters. "I was just checking in now that I'm on my way back."

"Back from where?" I ask him, turning away from Dante now that something more important has grabbed my attention. "You weren't supposed to finish your shift until midnight."

"Yeah, but that cop guy showed up and said he had his own guys coming in, and I could leave, so I left."

I turn to the others, puzzled. "Craig called him off. Said he was using his own guys."

"Since when does Craig make that kind of call?" Dante looks at me, but I have no answers.

"I'm gonna fucking call him and ask him right now." Like I need this shit. He doesn't decide who sits outside that apartment or when they do it.

"Wait!" Dante shouts, grabbing me by the shoulders as I end the call with Bruce. All the arrogance is gone, wiped from his face. "Motherfucker. I told him! I told him you two were in the Hamptons when he asked me how Emilia was fitting in around here."

His words land like a ton of bricks, flattening me, filling me with sickening dread. "He knew?"

His hands clamp down, almost crushing my joints, but I hardly feel it. "Oh, shit," he whispers, shaking his head. "I swear to God, I didn't think about it until now. I swear, Luca. I remember he asked a question, and I answered on reflex."

Craig knew we were in the Hamptons.

Craig pulled Emilia's detail without checking in.

He's with her. He has to be.

"How long has it been since you left her?" I demand as soon as the bubble of shock pops and reality rushes in to fill the void. I'm already running for the door before Bruce answers.

"Maybe ten minutes ago?" he replies. "I'm on the road now."

"Get your ass back there!" I shout, sprinting down the hall with Cesco and Dante on my heels. "Go straight up to the apartment and kick the fucking door down if you have to. Do not leave until I get there. Understood?"

Dante meets me as I reach my car. "We could call the cops. They'll get there faster than we will."

"And tell them what?" I counter as I throw myself behind the wheel. "A former detective might be in danger from a current detective on our payroll? And how would we know that? There's no fucking way to explain this. He'd talk his way out of it, anyway."

"It could save her," he argues.

Now he's concerned with saving her? I'd laugh if I had it in me. "If one of the other guys we pay gets word the cops were called out to her address, he could kill her to shut her up before they arrive," I fire back. The thought makes me sick, but I can't push it out of my head. Why didn't I see it? Why didn't I question his loyalty?

"We could make it in a half hour at this time of night," Cesco points out. He doesn't have the back door closed before I'm peeling away from the house at top speed. Thirty minutes? I'll make it twenty, if that.

"I'll try Craig," Dante suggests, already on his phone.

The guys at the gate barely get it open in time for me to fly through. His angry grunt comes as no surprise. "No answer."

"Here..." I hand him my phone. "... try Emilia. Keep trying her."

I slam my foot down on the gas, ignoring the blaring horns from other vehicles as I swerve through light traffic. "Bruce will get there," I grit out through clenched teeth as my heart thuds in my ears. "Then, we will."

And when we do, Craig will breathe his last.

18

EMILIA

The man in the long, black coat couldn't look more out of place if he tried. Not that there's anything particularly strange or unique about Craig as he sits on the sofa, but he doesn't belong. Like a bull in a china shop, only he's not rushing around and breaking things. Maybe it has something to do with his demeanor. The way he keeps rubbing his hands on his thighs and tapping his foot against the floor like a man with something on his mind.

"You probably don't want to watch this." I pick up the remote to turn off the new season of *The Great British Bake Off* show, I've been trying to catch up on. It's not like I've been paying attention ever since Guilia's call, anyway.

"It's fine. I don't care. It's actually kind of soothing." Not a minute after, he says that one of the contestants drops an entire bowl of batter on the floor while trying to get it into greased tins. "Oof. That sucks," he groans out, wincing.

"So what's up?" I prompt. Not that I mind the company. I don't, in fact, even if Craig happens to be the company. I've been alone in here for days. Being in the same room as another person is a refreshing change, never mind how strange it is that he won't take off his coat.

I turn to him, eyeing the coat, wondering what the deal is. "Is there something I can help you with?" I ask.

Some nameless emotion washes over his face, wrinkling his brow before it smooths out again. He wouldn't be a bad-looking guy if he weren't always either scowling or smirking, two expressions that have never been my favorite.

"It's been a crazy few months." His shoulders shake when he laughs. "I guess I don't need to tell you that."

"I'm still trying to remember the past few months," I remind him with a short laugh of my own. I don't feel like laughing, and there's nothing amusing going on, but I feel the need to match his energy. Very strange, intense energy. I can't put my finger on what it is strange about him. I only know something is.

"Do you want something to drink, maybe?"

I have to get off the sofa.

I have to leave the room.

I can't remember a time when someone has thrown me off the way he is tonight.

"Do you have any alcohol around here?" He stretches his legs out, crossing them at the ankles and making himself comfortable while still wearing his coat. "I could use a drink."

"I was thinking more along the lines of water or iced tea, but there should be some in the cabinet." Yes, maybe he does need a drink. Maybe that would calm him down a little bit.

"Don't put yourself out or anything," he insists as I make a short walk to the galley kitchen. I open the cabinet closest to the refrigerator and find a quarter of a bottle of bourbon, some rum, and a little amaretto.

"Bourbon?" I call out to him.

"Sure. Rocks, if you have some." I made a fresh tray of ice yesterday since there's nothing grosser than ice that's sat in a freezer for ages.

I return to the living room and hand him the glass, which he accepts with a brief grin. "Nothing for you?" he asks when he notices my other hand is empty.

"Oh, no. I'm fine." I wander to the windows overlooking the street and look out the way I did earlier. The black car is gone. The space is empty. "That's weird," I murmur to myself.

"What is?" Craig asks behind me.

He can't see my eyes rolling. "Oh, I was just thinking it's weird that the guard left without somebody else replacing them right away. That's how it usually is," I explain, looking up and down the street. I don't see any other familiar vehicles.

Why not?

I hear the ice rattling in the glass. "Oh, that's the problem I was talking about when I came in."

Now we're finally getting somewhere. I turn away from the window. "Did something happen?"

"I was going to come up and say hello, check in on you," he explains in an offhand sort of way that contradicts the uptight, nervous energy from earlier. "And whatever moron Santoro assigned down there didn't know who I was and didn't want to let me up here. We exchanged words, and he said he was going to call your boyfriend to straighten things out."

Why did it take me so long to see what's been wrong all the time? "How did you know I was here? What, is somebody at the house, keeping you posted on every move I make?" The idea stirs nausea in my gut. Why not take out an ad in the paper?

He flashes one of his trademark smirks before sipping his drink, sighing after he swallows. "In a way, yes. He wanted increased attention on your building and had to go through me. I have a small group of guys I know I can trust, so nothing has to run past the higher-ups. We sort of handle things quietly amongst ourselves."

Maybe I shouldn't, but I can't help myself. "You mean there's a bunch of you being paid off by the family?"

He snorts like it's funny but won't look at me now. He stares into his glass, swirling the ice around. "If that's how you want to see it."

"That's how it is."

"Are we going to go through this again?" Looking up at the ceiling, he groans. "That's not why I came here. I'm not trying to fight with you or have a pissing contest over who is or was the better cop. Everybody has to make choices." He leans over to place the glass on the coffee table. "Sometimes, those choices are very difficult to make. Sometimes, we feel cornered and end up doing things we never imagined being capable of."

"You're preaching to the choir," I remind him, thinking of Luca and me. I chose to be with him, and I chose to leave him. I can't remember making that first decision, but I sure as hell know leaving broke my heart, even if I knew it was the right thing to do.

He jumps a little when there's a knock at the door. "Expecting someone?" he asks with suspicion in his voice.

"No. I wasn't even expecting you." I feel a little more secure, having him in the apartment as I approach the door. "Who is it?" I call out and hate the tremor of fear in the question.

"It's Bruce. Let me in."

I exchange a look with Craig before he gets on his feet, scowling like he's got my back. I doubt Bruce would be a threat, but this is the first time any of my assigned guards have come up here. I'm trembling a little as I unlock and open the door.

Right away, he barges in, looking over the top of my head at Craig. "The boss wanted me to come up," he mumbles without taking his eyes off my guest.

"How come?" I ask, looking at Craig over my shoulder before returning my attention to the stern Bruce.

"I thought I told you to leave," Craig says.

Wait. That's not right. That's not how he described it to me. Then again, he didn't have to tell me every word they exchanged. I guess he means he told Bruce it was not necessary for him to be here anymore. It doesn't make sense.

"Yeah, and the boss told me to come back up here because it's not up to you." When Bruce folds his massive arms and lifts his chin, it's a pretty damn intimidating sight. He's a big guy, a wall of muscle.

"Okay, let's not argue about this." I give Bruce a pleading look. "I'm sure you can wait outside until shift change, right?"

He shakes his head ever so slightly, his gaze unwavering as he stares at Craig. "He said I should stay right here."

Why would he say that? "None of you guys have stayed in here with me yet," I point out, wrapping my arms around myself to contain a slight shiver that insists on running up my spine. Something is seriously off here. "Is there some kind of problem nobody wants to tell me about?"

Bruce looks like he's about to speak, but his mouth snaps shut before anything comes out. "Well?" Craig prompts over my shoulder. "Is there something wrong? What else did your boss tell you?"

Dread is an icy finger tracing its way down the back of my neck and raising the fine hairs there. Never in my life have I felt so much like I'm only witnessing half of a conversation. Like there's more going on underneath the words being spoken.

"That's none of your business," Bruce mutters. For a big guy, he's very agile, deftly placing himself between Craig and me. "Unless the boss says it is when he gets here."

"Luca's coming here?" The thought of it makes my pulse race, though I don't know if it's anticipation or dread causing it.

"He's on his way," Bruce grunts out, still facing Craig, who stands in the middle of my living room. That funny sheen of sweat has his face glistening again.

Suddenly, he withdraws a pistol from his holster. I barely have time to register the sight of it before a muffled gunshot makes me shriek and fall back against the wall while the mountain of muscles in front of me collapses.

"Oh my God!" It's pure reflex that makes me drop to my knees next to the wounded man as everything I ever learned about triage races through my skull. "Bruce, it'll be okay. Just stay with me."

It's a lie. He's coughing up blood thanks to the dark red stain rapidly growing across his chest. The sound of him choking on his own blood is horrible, but it's the way his widened eyes dart around like he's afraid that leaves me biting back a sob.

It's not until he releases one final, gurgling breath that I realize Craig sidestepped us and put the chain lock in place on the door before turning the bolt. He now stands with his back against it, still holding his gun. "I didn't want to have to do that," he murmurs, and there's almost regret in the statement.

The most incredible thing happens. In the time it takes my heart to beat, the horrible screaming in my head goes silent. The wild, racing thoughts go still. My awareness hardens, laser-focused.

"Why did you do that?" I question, kneeling next to Bruce, his blood coating my hands.

"He shouldn't have been here. He wasn't supposed to be," he says with a slight shrug. Maybe it's fear freezing me in place or disbelief. It doesn't matter which. Either way, I can't move as Craig slowly raises the gun, aiming it at my head.

"I don't understand." He doesn't try to stop me as I rise, my legs shaking. I don't take my eyes off him while options race through my head. I need a weapon. The kitchen is nearby, but he could easily put a bullet in me before I take a single step. I need to disarm him somehow if I'm going to get out of this.

"That asshole. That fucking asshole," he snarls out, sweating worse than ever now, his skin almost gray, his breathing harsh. "He had to go and fucking say something to you about me. He told me he did. After we found out you were still alive in the hospital. They were supposed to kill you that night, but somebody dropped the fucking ball." A high-pitched, almost crazy laugh bubbles out of him.

I don't remember much of this man, yet the sense of betrayal is still sharp, stinging, and bitter. "You aren't only working for the Santoro family, are you?" I whisper. "You were working for Vitali. That's how they knew where to find us. You told him."

"And he fucking told you about me!" he shrieks. "What, was I supposed to wait for you to remember?

Where does that leave me? Floating face down in the fucking Hudson, that's where... if your sweet Luca didn't cut me to pieces," he adds with a bitter chuckle. "Like I said. Sometimes, we face terrible choices. I didn't want to have to do this."

Luca is on the way. I only have to keep him from killing me until he gets here. When did he leave? How fast can he make it?

"I'm genuinely sorry for this." He takes one step toward me, then another. I back away on trembling legs, my heart pounding so hard I can barely hear him over the thundering noise. "Really," he insists as he steps over Bruce's body.

His gaze lowers to the floor, trying to avoid stepping in the blood, I realize, and I use the chance to make a run for it. Instinct takes me to the bathroom, where I lock the door before prying the lid from the top of the toilet tank.

"You think this is going to stop me?" Craig's voice rings out louder the closer he comes to the locked door. "You know I could shoot at this door until it's nothing but sawdust and be out of here in seconds. Honestly, I'd rather it be that way. I don't want to have to see you suffer."

"Because you're a spineless coward?" I creep back to the door, holding my breath. Slowly, I unlock the knob, praying he won't notice. "You know Luca sent Bruce here for a reason, right? He's on his way here. He knows what you did, and he's going to flay you alive for it."

Craig hesitates for a long, breathless moment before muttering, "He won't have proof." Then, a high-pitched whining sound fills my ears, and I only realize a second later that a bullet whizzed dangerously close to my head.

That's all it takes for everything to go red, for something dangerous and primal to be unleashed in me. I pull the door open, long enough to recognize Craig's slack-jawed surprise before I raise the porcelain lid to the side and swing for the fences.

"Fuck!" he shouts when I make contact with the hand holding the gun. The gun goes flying toward the living room before I swing again, but this time, he blocks the blow with an arm thrown in front of him. It's still enough to knock him back a step. I take advantage, darting past him, racing to reach the gun lying partway under the sofa.

"You little bitch!" he howls out. I'm almost there when something heavy knocks me to the floor and forces the breath from my lungs. It's Craig's body, and he rolls me onto my back while I gasp for air.

All of my self-defense training comes flooding back. I use it, kicking and scratching, determined to capture his DNA, if nothing else. If I manage to claw an eye out, all the better.

"It didn't... have to be... this way..." he growls out as we struggle, with him defending himself from my blows and me fighting to buck his much larger body off mine. I manage to drive a fist into his eye, which is almost enough to knock him off me, but when I stretch in a desperate attempt to reach the gun, he only closes his hands around my throat.

I remember reaching for a gun another time. In the bathroom. The gun was next to the toilet, just out of my reach the way it is now. The images overlap in my mind's eye, one after the other. Luca killing my assassin. The cabin.

What difference does it make when I'm about to die?

I can't die.

Not now.

Not like this.

The pressure against my throat increases, and I gasp, my eyes bulging, as Craig stares down at me. He's wild, insane, shaking, growling, and babbling while spit hits my face.

"Not my fault. Didn't want to do this," he insists, squeezing until everything starts to go gray, and I can't fight anymore. I can't breathe.

This is it. I'm going to die. I feel it. I hear the rattle in my throat.

Luca, I'm sorry. His image floats across my fading consciousness, and I grab onto it, holding it as my eyes close.

"What the fuck?" Craig's sudden shout comes at the same moment the pressure miraculously lessens and allows me to take a breath. Then a sharp crack fills the air, and Craig falls to my side, eyes wide and sightless, thanks to the gruesome hole in his temple.

Someone is holding me, lifting me until I'm sitting up and gagging, choking, fighting for every sip of air. "Oh, fuck, Emilia," someone gasps. "Oh my God."

It's Luca. Luca's arms, Luca's chest, Luca's voice in my ear. Luca, who I love. Luca, who saved my life again. Who stood up against his father and his family to keep me alive. He was ready to turn his back on everything, all for me.

I take one huge lungful of air after another, clutching Luca's shirt in my fists, soaking him in my tears. "I've got you," he tells me repeatedly, rocking me like a baby. "I've got you, baby. You're safe now. I love you. You're safe."

He needs to know. I have to tell him. Raising my head from his chest, I look into his dark eyes. "I remember." It comes out as a croak, something ugly and painful. "Everything. I remember. I love you."

He takes my face between his hands, laughing in disbelief. "You remember?"

My head bobs before I croak out three more words despite my raw throat. "Take me home?" Because now, I remember where I belong. I should have never left.

"We've got this," Dante mutters. I didn't realize until now that we aren't alone. Cesco is already pulling on gloves ready to clean up. "Take her home. We'll use Bruce's car to get back."

Luca helps me to my feet, and I lean against him, letting him lead me out. He could lead me anywhere.

I know who I am and where I belong for the first time in weeks.

19

LUCA

It's déjà vu in the best possible way.

Bringing her here again, I wasn't sure it would bring her unwanted memories, but witnessing her joy as we walk along the beach hand-in-hand made me realize she's made of stone and so much stronger than anyone I've ever known.

"I can't wait to bring you back here during the season," I tell her, pulling her close and placing a kiss against the side of her head. Her hair has started to come back, and I've heard Guilia talking about a pixie cut—whatever the hell that is. I then place another kiss on her hand over the scar, a permanent reminder of her ordeal. She doesn't believe me when I tell her she's beautiful no matter what her hair looks like, no matter what scars remain. It doesn't change who she is.

Who she is is someone whose return to my life has given me new purpose. I can imagine a future again. A reason to keep going. All thanks to her.

She leans against me and puts an arm around my waist. "I kind of like it now," she confesses. "Even if it's still a little chilly. I like feeling like we have the whole beach to ourselves."

"I know what you mean." However, I'm unable to resist her ass before winking. "Maybe I just want to show you off."

A devilish gleam touches her eyes when she grins up at me. "Oh, since you put it that way..." She's giggling by the time I take hold of her, lifting her off her feet and swinging her in a half circle dangerously close to the approaching surf.

It's magic, pure and simple. When we're here, I can let go of everything else. Granted, there are still guys watching us from a safe distance, and there will be until this bullshit with Vitali is settled.

Emilia must notice my change in demeanor when I set her on her feet, since she frowns up at me before cupping my cheek with one hand. "What is it?" she asks, searching my face.

I glance over my shoulder to where Vinny watches the area from further down the beach. "I was wondering how long it will be before we can loosen things up a little, that's all."

She nods, her brow crinkling. "You said your dad thinks things could get settled any day now, right?"

He did, but it does not make me feel better. Not that he would explain why he holds that belief. Even Dante is frustrated as fuck, swearing up and down. He doesn't know what our father has in mind. That might be the only slight consolation in the middle of all this. Knowing my brother is as deep in the dark as I am and how crazy it drives him.

We continue our walk, and I nod firmly, determined not to worry her. "He did. I believe him. Hopefully, he can work something out with Giorgio." Word has it Giorgio Vitali rallied after he got word of a few things his son was hiding from him, including his penchant for abducting and torturing young women. Not that the Vitali family ever shied away from violence, but there are lines we don't cross in our world. Like Papa, Giorgio is old-school. He believes in standards. What a shame he couldn't raise his son to give a shit about those values.

"Either way..." she concludes, "... we are okay. We are going to be fine. I'm not going anywhere."

"You don't need to keep reminding me of that." However, I do appreciate hearing it. Losing her was every nightmare come to life, and getting her back was the answer to prayers I don't deserve to have answered. I'm not a good man. I've done terrible things. Yet somehow, someone up there decided I deserved her.

"There won't come a minute when I don't treat this like a gift," I murmur mostly to myself while coming to a stop near the surf's edge, taking her hands in mine.

She offers a confused smile. The morning sunlight makes her eyes sparkle. "What do you mean?"

Great. Now that I've said it, I can't pretend I didn't. "There's a reason I'm better at writing letters than I am at saying these things out loud," I remind her with a wry chuckle.

"You're much better at expressing yourself than you think you are." She runs her thumbs over my fingers, grinning playfully. "Go on. Tell me what you meant."

"It's actually pretty simple." I draw nearer, my nose touching hers. She smells like vanilla and powdered sugar from our breakfast, and underneath it is a unique scent that belongs only to her. Delectable. "I lost you. I got you back, and I'm never going to take you for granted. Not for a single minute. I can't promise you're always going to like the things I do."

"I know," she whispers, but she hasn't pulled away. If anything, she leans in closer.

"So long as you always know they're *for* you. And hopefully, one day..." I trail off when my throat closes up.

A smile begins to stir the corners of her full mouth. "Yes? Complete the thought," she teases.

I might scowl, but I don't mean it. "You're going to bust my balls, aren't you? You're bound and determined," I growl out.

She looks down at my crotch, then back up at me. "Actually, I happen to like your balls the way they are."

"Yeah, you do." I brush my lips against hers, and her happy sigh makes me do it again. "But I mean it. One day, when we have a family, the things I do will be for them too. For all of us."

The box in my pocket feels heavier than it already did, which is saying something. The weight of the ring I've carried around countless times is almost enough to crush me. I've always heard the saying about something burning a hole in somebody's pocket, but I never considered it literally.

I have the whole night planned like I did before—dinner, champagne, and flowers. She deserves something special, something beautiful.

However, when I check in with my gut, this moment feels real. It feels right—the waves gently lapping at the shore, the two of us on the beach, nothing but sunshine and salt air. We might as well be the only two people on Earth when I gaze into her eyes, and she stares into mine.

"Marry me," I whisper, my forehead touching hers. "Be my wife. Marry me, Emilia Washington."

Her head snaps back slightly, eyes widening, her mouth falling open. "Did I hear that right?" she breathes out.

"You did." I can't believe I'm about to do something so corny, so unlike me, but she deserves this. She deserves the entire moment, beginning to end, which is what lowers me to one knee in the sand. Her hands are shaking, and tears well in her eyes.

"Oh my God," she whispers, smiling and crying at the same time.

"I was going to do this the first time we were here," I confess. "That was my plan. Giving you an amazing night, treating you like the queen you are. We're still doing that tonight," I add, and her head falls back so she can shout her laughter toward the sky.

"We don't need to," she insists, still giggling when she looks at me again.

"We will, but I couldn't wait," I conclude with a shrug. "It felt right... now, in this moment. I can't wait to tell you how completely and totally I love you. How committed I am to our future. And how I'd be the happiest, luckiest son of a bitch on Earth if you would be my wife. Will you? Will you marry me, Emilia?"

"You know I will." That's all she manages to get out before her tears turn to gusty sobs, dropping to her knees to throw her arms around my neck. This is more than enough. Right here, the two of us wrapped in each other, it's everything. All I will ever need.

"Oh, I forgot. Shit, I fucked it all up." I could kick myself as I fumble in my pocket before pulling out the box.

"You didn't fuck up anything," she insists, beaming. "This is all so beautiful."

I know she means it, but I'm going to do this the right way. "I've been carrying this around since before that first trip. My mother gave it to me for you."

Her teary eyes bulge when she takes her first look at the

ring. "Luca, it's gorgeous." She touches her shaking hands to her chest. "I can't believe it. So beautiful."

"Which makes it perfect for you." It slides easily over her ring finger, and the center diamond sparkles wildly in the sun. My heart swells when she holds her hand out to admire it, tilting it back and forth to catch the brilliant sparkles that remind me of the sparkling water beyond the sand.

"I love it. I love you." She takes my face in her hands and pulls me in for a deep, slow kiss that gives me no choice but to wrap my arms around her and clutch her tight against me.

When my stiffening dick presses against her, she releases a throaty groan before breaking the kiss to give me a wicked grin. "What a shame it's too cold to strip you naked here and now," she murmurs in a low voice.

"We're not far from the house," I remind her, groping her ass until she squeals and fights her way to her feet.

"Race you." She's already running by the time I stand, kicking sand up behind her, squealing and laughing. "Last one there has to go down on the other one first!"

Like that's an incentive to beat her, though I doubt I could if I tried. Some people are better at running in sand than others. Since I am nowhere near as fast as she is, she's waiting at the door by the time I reach the house, arms folded, her foot tapping. "I guess this means you have to pleasure me," she observes with a dramatic sigh.

Rather than answering words, I bend to throw her over my shoulder once I have the door unlocked. Her screams of laughter echo through the first floor as I carry her up the stairs, heading straight for the bedroom. I barely give her time to unzip her jacket when I've thrown her to the bed before I'm on her, my hands running over her body, unbuttoning her jeans, pulling off her shoes to peel the denim away from her soft legs and over her feet.

"What a shame you're such a fast runner." I toss my coat aside and tug off my sweater, but that's all I can manage to do before there's no choice except fall to my knees between Emilia's spread thighs. There's nothing I would rather do than run my tongue over her silky skin, inching my way closer to the place where she's hot and wet, where her aroma draws me in and promises the pleasure of her addictive pussy.

"How do you do this to me?" she whispers. I look up to find her head rolling from side to side while she runs her fingers through my hair. "One touch and I'm soaking wet."

She isn't lying. By the time I reach the crease between her leg and her plump, smooth lips, there is a wet spot spreading over her thong's crotch. I brush my nose over it, inhaling deeply, pulling her into my lungs, and letting her wreak havoc on my senses.

There's nothing in the world but this now. My entire focus is trained on her, on this. I peel away her thong and part her lips with my tongue, driving it deep, lapping as much of her wetness as I can before going back for more and more.

By the time I close my lips around her clit, she's moaning my name, her body undulating like the waves outside. I can't wait to spend the rest of my life doing this to her. Kissing, touching, and licking until she falls apart. I plan on making it my life's mission to unravel her every chance I get.

"Oh, fuck yes," she whimpers out between panting for air, scraping her nails over my scalp, holding my head close, and riding my face as pleasure takes over for everything else. She's losing herself, and it's because of me and what only I can do to her body. I can suck on her clit and caress her skin, and she's helpless. "Just like that," she begs, hips frantically jerking. "Make me come."

All I can do is obey and hang on for dear life when her hips begin to buck and her thighs close around my head, blocking out everything but the blood rushing in my ears. I can't help but chuckle as pride surges through me with the flood rushing from her when she explodes, screaming for me.

Instead of letting up, I work two fingers inside her tight channel, playing with her G-spot while her juices run onto my palm, and she continues moaning, writhing. "Come for me again," I growl out, reaching up with my free hand to play with her tits before flicking my tongue over her clit again. I want her to feel everything, to experience pleasure like she doesn't know exists. Because she's mine, she's agreed to always be mine, and that makes it my responsibility. I must be the luckiest man on Earth.

By the time she practically collapses against the mattress, flushed, glowing, and moaning hoarsely, I am painfully hard and aching to be free. "I need inside this pussy," I mutter as I kick off my shoes and shove my pants and boxer briefs down to my ankles. I'm dripping, so ready to sink in deep and let her consume me.

And when I do, when our bodies are locked together, and she wraps her arms and legs around me to draw me deeper, I know I'm home, where I belong and the only place I want to be. "I love you," I manage to whisper, kissing her before I begin to move before she begins to move with me.

Fuck, she's so tight. Made for me. And when I ride her hard, when I drive her into the mattress with every deep stroke, she takes it and begs me for more. "Yes... harder," she hollers, her nails running across my shoulders and making me hiss with pain that softens into pleasure, making my cock surge and my hips pump faster, driving harder the way she wants it.

"You feel so good," I groan out, closing my eyes, focused on the sensation of her pussy gripping me tighter, on the sloppy sound of her juices when our bodies crash together. Faster, harder, rutting like an animal until she arches against me and screams my name. Another few pumps, and I let go, pouring myself into her, giving myself over to what she does to me. I can't control it. I never could.

Not that I want to.

"I love you... fiancé," she whispers before giggling breathlessly. I push myself up on my forearms to find her grinning from ear to ear. "That sounds good, doesn't it?"

"Not quite as good as husband," I reply, rolling onto my back to smile up at the ceiling while she curls up next to me. "But I like the sound of it."

20

EMILIA

"You're sure this is okay?" Stepping back from the mirror, I run my hands over the front of the black sheath dress Giulia insisted I buy for tonight when we went shopping earlier. Sure, we had no fewer than three armed men shadowing us the entire time, but I wanted something special.

Luca steps up behind me, his hands on my hips, his lips grazing my neck before meeting my gaze in the glass. "You look incredible. You're stunning. Anyone would be happy to have you as their daughter-in-law."

He kisses my neck again before chuckling against my skin, and his hot breath somehow makes me shiver. "I can't say the same about your parents and me."

"They're going to come around." Reaching behind me, I cup the back of his neck, then turn my face toward his for a kiss. I still see the concern etched in the lines between his eyebrows. "Neither of them dropped dead when we called to tell them about the engagement, right? And they did agree to come here for dinner tonight. That's a big deal." So big. Huge. Terrifying.

The lines smooth out. "You're right. I hate to think of anything putting a shadow over this, is all."

"I love you for that." I love him for so many things, but that is definitely one of them. "There are no fairy tales. Nothing is ever totally perfect."

"Except for you," he insists, kissing the tip of my nose.

"You never miss an opportunity, do you?" I ask with a smile.

"Not if I can help it." His hands tighten with urgency, and he pulls me close, grinding against me a little and releases a low growl. "Speaking of opportunities..."

"Don't even think about messing up my makeup," I warn, and I'm not really kidding. I want to look perfect tonight. It doesn't help that I'm a little more anxious about my parents than I want him to know. If just one hair of my wig is out of place—I don't think they could handle seeing me without it—they'll immediately assume something is wrong. I know how their imaginations can run wild, especially Mom's. I won't give them the opportunity to get the wrong idea.

"You expect me to spend all night wanting you but keeping my hands off you?" he questions, staring at my mouth while he grinds against my ass. "When you look like a goddess?"

"You're just going to have to wait." After giving him a light, teasing little kiss, I add, "Anticipation makes it better, right?"

"So does bending you over this dresser and fucking the shit out of you here right now." He doesn't, though, stepping back and straightening out the front of his slacks before adjusting his tie and his cuffs. "I got a text from Guilia. Your mom and dad got here a few minutes ago."

"And you only told me now?" I squeal.

Suddenly, my stomach is churning, my hands are shaking, and I wish I had more time before we had to do this. I'm glad to see Mom and Dad, but I'm not looking forward to watching my parents silently judge everything and everyone around them.

Keeping the two halves of my family separate won't work forever. They're going to be spending time together eventually, so we might as well get them used to it now. Because at the end of the day, nothing is going to change the fact that Luca and I are meant to be. God knows we've been through enough, but we keep fighting our way out of it together.

One thing is for sure. I'm not going to leave them up there without me for long. "I guess we'd better get moving," I announce in a shaky voice.

Luca takes my left hand, where I feel the pressure of my ring. It's the most beautiful thing I've ever seen, much more beautiful than anything I ever dreamed of owning. Isabella almost wept with joy when we came back from the Hamptons, and she saw it on my finger. I wish I could say the same for my own mother, but I'm afraid the best I can hope for as we leave the house and make the short walk up to the mansion is for her to be on her best behavior.

As it turns out, I had nothing to worry about. The champagne has already been popped, and my parents are holding flutes, deep in conversation with Mr. and Mrs. Santoro when we enter the dining room. The table is set spectacularly with china, sparkling crystal, flowers, and candles. Something I didn't expect are the wrapped gifts stacked on the credenza and several bottles of champagne waiting on ice along with wine Rocco specially chose from the cellar in the basement. It's an intimate engagement party, but no less stunning.

"The happy couple!" Isabella chirps when she spots us.

"We were showing your parents around." Well, she sounds happy. I hope that means nobody has insulted her yet.

"Look at you." Mom's eyes shine with tears as she approaches, arms spread wide. "Glowing. You look radiant."

"Thank you. And thank you for coming," I whisper in her ear while we hug. "Thank you for doing this."

Dad kisses my forehead once she lets me go. "This is quite the showplace. I'm very impressed."

"And you haven't seen all of it yet. If you're interested, I'd love to show you around the wine cellar." Rocco is downright jovial, and I want to think the rosy color in his cheeks isn't entirely from champagne. A quick look at Luca reveals his relief at how healthy and vibrant Rocco seems tonight. Granted, this could be an act for my parents' sake, but considering how worried Luca has been for him, it's encouraging.

Rocco takes my hand and wears what seems to be a genuine smile. "Emilia, sweetheart. You look very lovely. You should know before you came in, your mother and my wife were already deciding the date of the wedding." He winks broadly, chuckling.

"We did no such thing!" Isabella chides him with a gentle, playful slap against his shoulder. "We were only talking about the best times of year. And if the kids are going to be married anywhere half decent, we need to plan ahead. You can't simply call up and arrange for a wedding the following weekend."

"We haven't thought about any of that yet," I inform everyone, giggling nervously at the attention but more at how well things are going. I can't help it. Everything feels too perfect.

Should I be waiting for the other shoe to drop?

Maybe all of the shoes have already dropped. Maybe

that's how I need to think about it. We've been through all the bad stuff and cleared all the hurdles. It's nothing but smooth sailing from here.

"Well, you better start thinking about it," Mom insists. "There are so many things to be done. Trust me. You'll think you have all your bases covered until you realize how much you never thought of until it's too late."

Luca and I exchange a nervous glance. "How does Vegas sound to you?" he asks, and I have to laugh when Mom groans and Isabella mutters something sharp in Italian.

"Sister!" Guilia tears into the room like the whirlwind she is, wearing the cute, silver strapless dress she bought today. "I told you you'd look like a million bucks in this!" When she whirls her finger overhead, I give her a twirl before introducing her to my parents, who seem instantly taken with her. How could they not be? She ought to be the family ambassador. Nobody could resist her warmth and charm.

It isn't long before the room is full, and even Dante seems to be in a decent mood. I would like to believe that's because he's warming up to me, but I get the feeling it's more about putting on a show for the civilians. For him, it's all about image. I guess that's the sort of thing you have to worry about when you're the underboss. All I know is he was with Luca when they came on the run to stop Craig before he killed me. The bruises around my throat are gone, but the memory remains.

Guilia and our moms are discussing wedding dress designers by the time we take our seats for dinner. Isabella agreed to have it catered and served by hired staff so she could enjoy another miraculous event. "I don't need anything over the top," I insist, but it seems like my opinion is the one that means the least. Since when is the bride the last person anybody consults?

Not that I would complain, especially when Mom and Isabella are hitting it off so well. Dad is discussing golf with Rocco until Dante pipes up with something or other about football. Suddenly, the conversation moves in an even more animated direction. Nico and Francesco chime in occasionally with an opinion, though I get the feeling they're more interested in the people who bet money on the games than the games themselves. Still, they're on their best behavior along with everybody else.

"I'm starting to think this might actually work," I whisper to Luca. We're the only people at the table not involved in the conversations. We may as well be on our own.

"Don't say that too loud," he warns with a playful twinkle in his eyes. "You might jinx it."

"We deserve this." I mean it with all my heart and believe it with every bit of me. It's time for us to move into a happy future together.

By the time the almost overflowing platters have been placed on the table, and the room is full of the aromas of garlic, tomatoes, beef, and sausage, the staff has filled our wine glasses. Rocco holds his glass and stands at the head of a table. "I want to thank everyone for being here tonight," he begins in his gruff voice. "These are the moments that make everything worthwhile... having the family together, planning for the future, and celebrating the happy moments. I've been fortunate enough to spend most of my life with a true partner by my side. Someone who has created a beautiful life for me and our children."

Rocco's gaze softens when it rests on his wife before he turns his attention to us. "Luca, I truly believe you have found such a partner in Emilia. I hope you two can be even half as happy as we've been together."

How far we've come. I don't think anybody would ever have imagined him delivering such a lovely, heartfelt toast only months ago, back when he wanted me dead. I understand it wasn't personal, though I still wouldn't consider him my best friend. But we've come a long way.

It's obvious Luca is touched as he raises his glass to his father. "Thank you, Papa," he murmurs while I blink back grateful tears. This entire night is a dream come true. Having everybody here to celebrate us and help us plan for the future.

Just when I think Rocco is about to end the toast so we can eat, he continues. "While I do not wish to overshadow the happy couple's engagement party, I can't let the night go by without announcing that Luca is not the only Santoro son engaged to be wed." He looks around the table, smiling wide.

Wait a second. Why did I never hear anything about this? I look at Luca, ready to ask why the hell he never told me his brother is engaged, but he seems just as confused and surprised as I am. His mouth hangs open as he looks from Rocco to Dante and back again.

I notice the way Rocco's gaze brushes over my parents before he continues. "I am so happy to tell you the business problems we've been having lately have come to a resolution. It's over. Our family and the Vitali family are no longer at odds. As of this morning, we hope to move forward in an era of peace and prosperity."

Mom can't stifle a gasp. I have no doubt she's heard all about the war on the news—at least, the parts that made the news.

I find Luca's hand under the table and squeeze it tight,

but he doesn't react. Instead, he asks Rocco, "What did you do? When did this happen?"

"Is this for real?" Nico murmurs, sitting on Luca's other side.

Rocco is beaming as he claps a hand down on Dante's shoulder. "Family, before the year's end, Dante will be married to Giorgio Vitali's daughter, and our families will be united."

I don't know who looks more shocked. Luca, whose mouth still hangs open. Isabella, who's clutching her pearls in mute surprise? Guilia, whose eyes are bulging as she stares at Dante?

Or Dante himself, who very much looks like this is the first time he's heard about any of this?

"I can't believe it." Luca's mind is still miles away when he joins me in bed hours after the party ends. Here I am, naked and ready for him, but for once, something looms larger in his mind. "He went behind our backs and arranged a marriage. I never thought I'd feel sorry for Dante."

"Tell me the truth." I hook a leg over his hip, grinning playfully. "You liked watching your brother sputter and stutter like he did."

He can't help himself. A laugh bursts out of him, and I have to join in. I mean, the guy was determined to kill me, and he didn't bother hiding his feelings even as I stood in front of him. I'm not exactly going to weep over his arranged marriage.

Besides, it means ending the war. Life for us is never going to be normal—not by any definition I was raised with —but now, it can settle into a regular rhythm. We'll still be guarded, but we can come and go more freely without the fear of a Vitali assassin lying in wait. Guilia just about exploded with excitement at the idea of having her life back.

"Everything is falling into place." I use my fingertips to brush a strand of hair away from his forehead, then run my hand down his cheek. The feel of his skin never fails to electrify me. My core warms instantly, and my body wiggles closer to his without my meaning to. "We're going to have a beautiful wedding and a beautiful honeymoon. A beautiful life."

Any remaining tension flows from him under the spell of my touch until he's stirring against my hip and pulling me against him with a sexy growl. "How could we not, when you're part of it?" he asks with equal parts affection and desire in his voice.

Soon, all thoughts of the family fade into the background until it's just us. The way it was always meant to be.

THE END.

WANT MORE?

Did you know there are more Elite Men coming?

Head over to Missy's Website or any good book retailer to find out more.

ALSO BY MISSY WALKER

*Forbidden Lust/Love are a duet and to be read in order.

*Cruel Lust is a trilogy and to be read in order

All other books are stand alones.

JOIN MISSY'S CLUB

Hear about exclusive book releases, teasers, discounts and book bundles before anyone else.

Sign up to Missy's newsletter here:
www.authormissywalker.com

Become part of Missy's Private Facebook Group where we chat all things books, releases and of course fun giveaways!

https://www.facebook.com/groups/missywalkersbookbabes

ACKNOWLEDGMENTS

Huge thanks to my editing crew for their keen insights and invaluable guidance.

To my beta readers, your feedback is like uncovering hidden gems, even if it means braving a mountain of revisions afterward.

A big thanks to all my awesome fans for sticking with me through thick and thin and for always leaving such amazing reviews. You guys seriously fill my bucket! I'm all about crafting stories that whisk you away from the chaos of everyday life, and I truly appreciate every minute you spend diving into my books. Rest assured, I'm on a mission to deliver captivating reads that give you the perfect escape you're looking for.

And finally, my 'Babes!' in my Facebook group. At Missy Walker Book Babes, you guys seriously make me laugh. I love reading every single comment and post you guys make, and even more so I love this little reading community we have built together.

Stay tuned, everyone. There's plenty more excitement on the horizon.

Missy x

ABOUT THE AUTHOR

Missy is an Australian author who writes kissing books with equal parts angst and steam. Stories about billionaires, forbidden romance, and second chances roll around in her mind probably more than they ought to.

When she's not writing, she's taking care of her two daughters and doting husband and conjuring up her next saucy plot.

Inspired by the acreage she lives on, Missy regularly distracts herself by visiting her orchard, baking naughty but delicious foods, and socialising with her girl squad.

Then there's her overweight cat—Charlie, chickens, and border collie dog—Benji if she needed another excuse to pass the time.

If you like Missy Walker's books, consider leaving a review and following her here:

instagram.com/missywalkerauthor
facebook.com/AuthorMissyWalker
tiktok.com/@authormissywalker
amazon.com.au/Missy-Walker
bookbub.com/profile/missy-walker

Printed in Great Britain
by Amazon